IN TROUBLE WITH THE CLAW

A WHISKERS AND WORDS MYSTERY, BOOK 4

ERYN SCOTT

KRISTOPHERSON
PRESS
Publishing

Could Lou be *falling* right into the killer's trap?

Louisa's first fall in Button is everything she hoped it would be: corn mazes, pumpkin patches, quirky town traditions, and beautiful foliage. The only unexpected thing: a dead body found in a pile of colorful leaves.

When Lou starts getting text messages about the murder, she's wary, to say the least. Are the clues from the murderer baiting her into a trap? Or are they from someone who truly wants to help? When Lou is targeted as a suspect in the case, she may not have a choice but to listen. The mystery texter might be the only one who can help prove her innocence.

Welcome to Button

1 - Whiskers and Words   4 - George's Technology Emporium   7 - Button Bistro

2 - Material Girls   5 - Bean and Button Coffehouse   8 - Pet Store   9 - Bakery

3 - Willow and Easton's houses   6 - The Upholstered Button   10 - Old Mansion

11 - Willow's Nursery

CHAPTER I

Louisa Henry was of the opinion that there was no better combination of sounds than those in her bookshop.

She loved the quiet shuffle of books sliding off shelves as patrons took chances on new stories. The papery flip of a page signaled a reader might be poring over the first lines of text or possibly checking to see if there was a map. A wooden floorboard creaking indicated a reader walking slowly up one aisle and down the next. The cast-iron stove in the corner clicked like a metronome as orange-and-yellow flames danced inside, radiating heat into the shop. Mixed with those sounds sat the low hum of whispered conversation as two customers shared favorite sections from a series they loved.

Lou's bookshop was special, however, because it contained more than just the standard bookshop sounds; there were cat sounds too. Whiskers and Words was a bookstore that doubled as a rescue-cat sanctuary. Lou felt the sounds added by the cats only enhanced the peaceful atmosphere.

The deep, contented sound of purring filled the space as

the cats curled up throughout the shop. Soft paws padding along the worn wood floors were such a contrast to the heavy human footsteps. A happy meow might punctuate everything now and then as a feline circled someone's feet, waiting to be picked up.

Those were the noises that made up the soundtrack of Lou's day-to-day life, ever since she'd bought the bookstore and moved to the small town of Button ten months earlier.

Fall was turning out to be especially cozy inside Lou's book-shop. While dead leaves scurried down the chilly streets and tiny droplets of rain misted through the air, she was warm inside with her many cats and shelves upon shelves of books.

Closing her eyes, Lou wrapped herself in the sounds of her shop, as if they were a fluffy blanket wrapped around her shoulders.

That was, until a hiss, growl, and a scream of pain rang through the space.

Lou's eyes flew open, and she jumped up from where she'd been perched behind the register. Her gaze locked on a middle-aged woman with long dark hair pulled up into a ponytail, standing over a white cat. The woman clutched at her left arm. The cat crouched defensively on the table where he usually napped. The white cat, Sapphire, was not only Louisa's personal pet, but he was also deaf. He wore a collar with the words *Not for adoption* printed along it, so customers knew he'd already found his forever home.

There was also a sign sitting next to his favorite napping spot that explained his deafness. The sign informed people to tap on the table until he woke in order to avoid startling him.

The middle-aged woman clutching her forearm had obviously *not* heeded the sign's suggestion.

Still, surprise jolted through Lou's brain as it caught up with the scene in front of her. Sapphy hadn't attacked anyone since he was a feisty kitten.

Lou raced over, an apologetic frown securely in place. "I'm so sorry. He's never done anything like that here. He must've been startled." Lou pointed out the sign. "He's deaf."

The woman carefully peeled her hand away from her forearm like she expected blood to spurt out of the cut. The thin scratch was about three inches long. To any cat owner, such a scratch was to be expected every now and then—a small price in exchange for the company of the wonderful, sometimes temperamental, creatures.

But from the way the woman's mouth was contorted into a grimace, she acted as if it might lead to amputation.

"I don't care *what* he is. He's feral and dangerous." The woman's gaze flashed up to meet Lou's. "How dare you keep such an unpredictable animal in a public space. I could contract a disease from a cut like this."

Lou took a step back in surprise. Her frown deepened past an apology and into an argument. "Again, I'm sorry that he hurt you, but there is a sign next to him stating the correct way to wake him and avoid accidents such as this." Lou hadn't spent two decades living in New York City without learning how to stand her ground.

In order for Sapphire to have reacted as he had, the woman must've latched on to him with no warning, causing him to feel scared and defensive. Sapphire had been around children who weren't always gentle, and he'd never lashed out in such a way.

The woman flicked her long ponytail over one shoulder and scoffed. "You're trying to blame this on me?" She let out a humorless laugh. "Nice try. This is negligence of the worst kind. You haven't heard the last of me. I'm going to file a complaint with the county, and I'll make sure they euthanize this dangerous animal, so he doesn't attack anyone else." With that, the woman pivoted and stormed off.

A cold burst of air flooded into the bookshop in her wake, but it was nothing compared to the icy chill of fear she'd left behind in Lou's heart. Sapphire, sitting innocently on the table, blinked his jewel-toned blue eyes at Lou and cocked his head to the side as if asking, "What just happened?"

Lou scooped him into her arms and held him tight. "Don't worry, buddy. That mean woman won't do anything to you. I'll make sure she can't," she said, more to herself since he wouldn't hear a word of it.

Setting the cat back on the table, Lou became acutely aware that the handful of customers in the bookshop were all staring in her direction. They stood there open-mouthed as if they still couldn't believe the scene they'd just witnessed.

"Don't worry about Nina," Silas, one of Lou's regulars, said from his seat on the couch in the sitting area. "She'll calm down."

Nina. Lou hadn't ever met the unpleasant woman, though that wasn't a surprise, given that she'd only lived in the small Pacific Northwest town for less than a year.

"Is she always that unpleasant?" Lou asked, pushing her shoulders back as she walked behind her register computer.

Silas shook his head. "She's usually quite charming, actually. She's an accountant and helps me and some other residents with our taxes each year," he said, referring to Button House, the assisted-living community where he had a small apartment.

The other customers nodded their agreement, a few supplying their own examples of Nina's kindness.

"She helped my brother set up a retirement account and was fantastic at explaining the ins and outs to him," a woman said as she passed by on her way to the romance section of the bookstore.

A man cleared his throat. "My parents' business was struggling, and she taught them how to use a financial software program that's helped them watch their spending and even put money into savings."

Lou's anger dwindled as she questioned her outrage. It sounded like everyone genuinely liked this Nina woman.

"Maybe she's just having a bad day and took it out on Sapphy," Lou said, trying to assume the best of the frustrating situation.

"That's probably it," Silas said. "Trust me. She'll calm down, and I bet there will be no hard feelings tomorrow."

A long inhale calmed Lou the rest of the way. "You're probably right." She glanced around the shop, searching for a task on which to expend the excess energy that had built up from the adrenaline after her encounter.

"It might not be a bad idea to bring her a little peace offering to speed up the process." Silas winked at Lou. "She lives in the blue house on the corner of Pattern Drive and Bobbin Road."

Thanking Silas for the information, Lou checked on Sapphire. He was curled back into a ball, one small white paw hanging off the stack of books he slept on. The cat seemed no worse for wear after the encounter.

She supposed it wouldn't be the worst idea to apologize.

Lou closed the bookshop at lunch the next day. This was a normal occurrence since weekends were so busy with tourists, Lou didn't dare close the shop then, knowing she'd miss out on too much business. She still needed a break, however, so she closed early on Mondays and Tuesdays. That particular Monday, however, closing early felt more like a punishment than a break because she'd made the decision to spend her free time following Silas's advice and apologizing to Nina.

After putting together an apology basket and fussing with it for as long as she could, Lou climbed into her new car. Lou had never needed her own car when she lived in New York City. Even upon arrival in Button, Lou found the town compact enough that she could walk most places.

But as they headed into fall, and rain became a daily occurrence, Lou had seen the benefits and purchased her first new car. She loved the sporty little hatchback and couldn't help but smile each time she climbed behind the wheel.

Well, except this time. As Lou readied herself to apologize to Nina, even her car couldn't seem to cheer her up.

Lou drove over to the corner of Pattern Drive and Bobbin Road, stopping in front of the blue house. As she climbed out of her car, Lou balanced a basket of items she'd purchased from the bakery across the street as well as two bestsellers from the new-release table at the bookshop.

Lou pushed back her shoulders and walked up the concrete pathway leading to Nina's house. Being the middle of the day on a Monday, Lou figured—or hoped—that Nina would be at work. If she could apologize without having to interact with Nina, that would be even better.

Nina's small yard was covered in crisp orange and red leaves that had been previously attached to the maple trees on either side of the walkway. The way the leaves were strewn about reminded Lou of how a teenager's room might be littered with clothes they'd worn that week—or month.

The house was well kept, and the small porch looked like a

pleasant place to sit and observe the falling leaves while the neighborhood children rode by on their bicycles. Lou rang the doorbell and waited. She couldn't hear any movement inside. Trying a few sharp knocks on the door this time, Lou waited again. Still nothing.

Lou straightened the small card containing her apology, making sure it was easy to see, before placing the basket on Nina's doorstep. Just as Lou placed her foot on the first porch step, a gust of wind sent rain splattering onto the porch. Small droplets of rain darkened the envelope of the card sitting in the basket. While Lou had expected Nina might be at work, she hadn't expected this amount of wind to ruin her plan of leaving the basket behind.

If I leave that there, the card is going to get soggy. Even worse, those books might get wet.

That wouldn't work. Retrieving the basket, Lou walked back down the garden pathway and took a right, heading for the sage-green house next door. Unlike Nina's yard, this one had been raked free of leaves, though it held the same number of maple trees on either side of a similar walkway.

Lou rang the doorbell and waited. This time, someone came to the door.

The resident was a rather large man in both girth and height. He had rosy cheeks, and Lou would've bet anything that he was the owner of a lovely baritone laugh.

"Hello," he said, studying Lou for clues about why she was on his doorstep. His gaze landed on the basket in her arms.

She wet her lips. "Hi. I'm Louisa. I own the bookshop in town."

At this information, the man's quizzical expression softened into a smile. It was the kind of grin that only a true booklover adopted whenever they heard mention of a bookstore. Lou liked him immediately.

She jabbed a thumb toward Nina's house. "I wanted to leave this for Nina but she doesn't appear to be home. Would it be possible for me to leave it with—"

"Absolutely not," the man said, interrupting Lou. The kind expression he'd assumed at the word *bookshop* hardened into stone, and he looked like he might spit fire. "There's no way I'm helping that terrible woman."

Lou sucked in a surprised breath. She hadn't had the best interaction with Nina, but other locals seemed to like her. It was interesting to meet another person who disliked her so intensely.

"Oh, um ... okay." Lou took a step back, gripping the basket tighter.

As if the man realized he was scaring her, he held out a hand, palm forward. "I'm sorry. Nothing against you, but that woman's been more of a pain in my side than a burst appendix. I wouldn't help her if she was drowning." He stepped back into his house, letting the screen door slam shut behind him. "If I were you, I'd think twice about having more interactions with her than you need to." With that, he shut his front door.

Lou swallowed, processing what had just happened for a moment, as she stood, stunned, on the man's porch. Finally, she left his house. The rain was picking up; gusts were practically moving the precipitation sideways now, so setting the basket on the porch was still not an option.

"Maybe the other neighbor will hold this for her," Lou mused as she walked past Nina's house and turned left.

The house behind Nina's was painted a cream color, and Lou walked toward it. On this side of Nina's house, an enormous pile of leaves had been gathered, leaving a mound almost as tall as Lou. It caught Lou by surprise since Nina's yard didn't appear to have been raked at all.

Sticking to her mission, Lou carried on. She walked up Nina's backyard-neighbor's porch steps and knocked on the door. Again, no answer. They weren't home either. Lou's posture sagged. She was going to have to come back some other time.

Heading back to her car, Lou noticed a small dog playing in the pile of leaves in Nina's yard. Lou knelt so she might be less intimidating to the dog, who shied away once he noticed her.

"Hey, there, little one," Lou cooed at the fluffy dog. It looked like a Pomeranian, all white-and-black fluff.

The dog barked at Lou, then continued to dig in the leaves.

"Who do you belong to?" Lou stood, checking over each shoulder to see if there were any people searching for a lost dog.

The streets were empty. Everyone was tucked away inside, safe and warm against the chilly fall weather. Lou wanted to do the same, a mug of tea and a good book sounding perfect just about now. But she couldn't leave this little dog out in the cold either.

Hooking the basket on one arm, Lou stepped into Nina's yard, toward the dog. But as she rounded the pile, Lou noticed something sticking out of the leaves that she hadn't seen the first time she'd walked past.

A hand and part of a forearm stuck out from the bottom of the pile. The little dog had moved the leaves enough to uncover it.

Lou gasped. The basket in her arms dropped to the ground with a sickening thud.

And as she caught sight of the red scratch, about three inches long, running down the pale forearm, Lou had a terrible feeling she knew who was buried under those leaves.

CHAPTER 2

Fingers shaking, Lou pulled out her phone and called emergency services. The small dog watched her, his head tipping from side to side as she explained where she was and what she was looking at.

"Is the person breathing?" the dispatcher asked. "Can you feel a pulse?"

Lou grimaced as she leaned closer to the arm. With shaking fingers, she reached forward and placed her fingertips on the wrist. The skin was cold, and even after waiting seconds, Lou couldn't feel anything resembling a pulse.

"Nothing," Lou whispered in defeat, sitting in the wet grass.

"Okay. I'm sending a police unit and paramedics your way," the dispatcher said.

Lou let the phone drop into her lap as she ended the call. As if the phone had been an invitation, the dog trotted over and curled into her lap as well. It rested its head on her knee.

"Oh, little buddy." Lou pushed out her bottom lip. "Where's your home?" She studied its collar, which was pink and sparkly. "Mr. Muffins?" She read the name on his tag.

The dog lifted his head in recognition and considered Lou.

Flipping the tag over, Lou's blood ran cold. The name and address on the back confirmed her suspicion that this little canine belonged to Nina Upton.

"No wonder you were hanging around this pile of leaves," Lou said, scooting back a few inches and pulling the dog into a hug. "That's your owner in there. I'm so sorry."

Mr. Muffins flinched as a car door slammed. Lou turned to see an EMT vehicle from the fire department parked on the street corner, lights flashing in warning to those around. With the emergency vehicle's arrival, neighbors ventured out into the cold weather, standing on porches or peering through open windows to see what was happening.

As Lou stood to greet the paramedics, a black sedan pulled up in front of her. A man with dark hair and a grim expression climbed out of the driver's side. He wore a detective's badge and a scowl that he directed at Lou.

She regarded the man with surprise, having expected the tall, blond Detective Easton West. Lou had been to the local police station a few times—more than she'd ever expected in the short time she'd lived in Button—and had met a few of the other officers but had never noticed another detective besides Easton.

The mystery detective leveled her with a no-nonsense stare as he approached. Mr. Muffins struggled in her arms, telling Lou she wasn't the only one intimidated by this man. Lou held the dog more securely, which seemed to calm him because he stopped squirming.

"Hi, I'm Louisa. I called this in." She shifted the dog so he was tucked under her arm and held out her right hand to the detective.

He regarded her outstretched hand, not making any movement toward shaking it.

"I'm Detective Roy Anderson with the Button Police Department." Roy's gaze landed on the arm hanging out of the pile of leaves. "Do you want to explain to me what happened here?" he asked in a tone that almost sounded accusatory.

Lou pulled her hand back, overcoming her surprise. "Well," she said, not sure where to start, "I came by to drop off this basket." Lou gestured to the basket of books and baked items she'd dropped in the grass when she'd noticed the body.

"Why?" Detective Anderson asked.

Lou wrinkled her nose for the briefest of seconds. She cleared her throat. "Nina ..." She pointed to the house. "The woman who lives here, who I believe is in *there*"—Lou nodded toward the pile of leaves—"came into my bookshop, Whiskers and Words, yesterday," she explained, watching him for any hint of recognition.

Detective Anderson stared at her, not even giving her so much as a blink.

Lou continued. "So Nina came into my shop yesterday, and besides selling books, I also have several cats in the shop. Most of them are up for adoption, but my personal cat, Sapphire, is deaf. I have signs posted around him, letting customers know they should approach him carefully and tap on nearby surfaces to wake him before petting him." Detective Anderson looked increasingly bored by her story, so Lou rushed to get the last bit out. "Nina must not have read the sign. He got scared and scratched her." Lou used her index finger of her free hand to draw a three-inch line on the skin of the arm she held Mr. Muffins with. Then she eyed the scratch on the arm sticking out of the leaf pile.

Detective Anderson followed her gaze, then turned his glare back at Lou, waiting for the rest of her story.

"We both overreacted to the situation, so I brought her a basket today, to apologize," Lou said, her discomfort rising with each passing second.

The paramedics, who'd already checked for signs of life, removed the leaves to expose Nina's body. There was no doubt she was dead, from the way her eyes and mouth were open and the thin mark around her neck like the choker necklaces Lou and her best friend, Willow, used to wear in middle school. Lou swallowed as she recognized Nina was also wearing a matching flannel pajama set. She must've been killed during the night or early in the morning.

Letting her body give in to the shiver it felt at the sight of Nina's body, Lou said, "Yeah. That's Nina Upton, the woman I came to see." Then, when the detective said nothing, she asked, "Where's Easton?" Lou hoped the other detective was just out of town for the day.

Detective Anderson narrowed his eyes. "Detective West is dealing with a different case. You're stuck with me. Sorry." Sarcasm dripped from the word. "So, you're telling me you had a fight with this woman yesterday? And now she's dead in a pile of leaves in her yard."

"'Fight' might be an exaggeration," Lou said, feeling sweat gather on her temples despite the chilly temperature outside.

"Then what would you call it?" Detective Anderson asked.

"A misunderstanding?" Lou tried.

"Do you know many murderers return to the scene of the crime after the victim is already dead?" He met her gaze.

Lou's lips parted. "I did not know that," she said, even though she actually did.

The detective's gaze moved over her like a metal detector

might scan a body. "Sometimes it's because they want to double-check they didn't leave anything behind. You know, clean up their tracks." He cocked an eyebrow at her. "Sometimes they want to be the ones to 'discover' the body, so it doesn't seem like they could've possibly been the one to kill them. Is that what you're doing?"

"What?" Lou spat out the question before she could stop herself. "You can't possibly think I had anything to do with this."

He moved his head back in surprise. "Oh, I can't, can I? Thank you for telling me how to do my job."

Lou opened her hands, then closed them again as if grasping for sanity and reason but finding none in the space between them.

"Did you or did you not get into an argument with this woman within the last twenty-four hours?" Detective Anderson asked.

"Yes, but... Ask my customers. They were there. They'll tell you—" She stopped herself, remembering how everything had gone down yesterday. If he asked her regulars, they would tell him all about Nina threatening to have Lou's beloved cat euthanized.

That wouldn't look good for her since the detective already suspected her, and he didn't even know the worst parts. She clamped her mouth shut and figured saying nothing more was her best bet.

Detective Anderson swept his dark hair back so it was off his forehead. "You better believe I'll be talking to anyone who witnessed that fight. Don't worry."

Lou sank her fingers into Mr. Muffin's long fur to combat the shiver that prickled at her skin. "Do you need me to stick around any longer, or can I go?"

He exhaled through his nose so it sounded a little like a snort. "Go ahead. But don't leave town. I'll definitely have more questions for you."

"Where would I go?" Lou asked rhetorically. "I own a shop in town. I live here."

Button was finally becoming her home, her sanctuary. Right now, however, it felt like a prison.

Instead of saying anything more, Detective Anderson continued to inspect her, causing an eerie chill to settle over her. He looked at her like someone might look at a killer.

"What should we do about her dog?" Lou asked, scanning her surroundings as if an answer might present itself. But all she could see were paramedics and crime scene technicians, all with jobs to do.

The detective rolled his eyes. "Just leave it here. I'll have animal control come take care of it."

Lou trusted that statement about as far as she could throw the man. Also, a worry tingled at the back of her mind at his wording. *Take care of it?* That didn't sound good.

"Why don't I call Dr. Romero?" she offered, mentioning her friend Noah, the local veterinarian. "He'll know what to do."

Detective Anderson shrugged as if he couldn't care less. Then he turned toward the death scene and checked in with the forensic team.

Lou's phone was already in her pocket from her call to 9-1-1. As she dialed Noah's number, she hoped he would be available. It was the middle of a workday for him, and he might be swamped at the clinic.

"Hey, Lou," Noah answered after a couple of rings. "What's up?" He sounded easy and conversational as if she might've found another stray cat she needed him to come check out.

Just hearing his voice made her feel calmer.

"So…" she started, not sure how to transition into her news. "I have a dog that needs a home, and I'm wondering if you can help."

"A dog?" he asked in surprise. Lou didn't blame him, since they were used to talking about cats. "Where'd you find it?"

Lou shuffled her feet in discomfort as she realized she was going to have to come out with the truth. "That's the thing. It's Mr. Muffins, Nina Upton's dog. And he's going to need a home because … she's dead."

A fresh gust of biting fall wind moved through the street, cutting through Lou's jacket and chilling her to the bone.

CHAPTER 3

Noah was silent on the other end of the call for a few moments.

"Did you hear me?" Lou asked. "Nina's dead. Do you know her dog, Mr. Muffins?"

"Sorry, yes," Noah said after a beat. "You caught me by surprise. I know Mr. Muffins very well. Where are you?"

Worry encompassed Lou. Noah knew the dog. Had he known Nina? Was she a friend? If so, no wonder he'd needed a second after she'd dropped that terrible news on him like a cup of scalding coffee right into his lap.

"Noah, I'm so sorry," she said instead of answering his question. "I didn't mean to be so crass. Were you close with her?"

There was an audible sigh before Noah answered. "No need to apologize. I only knew her through her dog and his *many* vet appointments."

"Okay. I'm at Nina's house," she finally answered. "Do you know where that is?"

Lou was tempted to vent about the situation with the sour Detective Anderson, but she didn't even know where to start. Explaining that it seemed like she was the prime suspect in Nina's murder would probably be best done in person.

"Oh, sure. I live a few doors down, actually," Noah said in surprise. "I came home to grab lunch. I'll be right there."

The knowledge that her friend would be there any moment made the tension she'd been holding in her shoulders release. That feeling was nothing compared to seeing Noah walking down the street toward where she stood, still clutching Mr. Muffins like she was the lost pet and needed his help, instead of the other way around.

Noah wore an orange-and-brown flannel shirt that, along with his dark hair and beard, made him look more like he was about to chop down a tree in the woods than tend to the medical needs of an animal. His brown eyes crinkled with worry as they met Lou's, asking questions before he could even reach her.

"Are you okay? What can I do to help?" Noah placed a gentle but strong hand on Lou's arm, holding her gaze with his.

"I'm okay. Nina ... not so much." Lou jerked her chin toward the active investigation behind her. "I think she was strangled."

Noah took it all in, scanning the leaves, the body, the police presence.

"Mr. Muffins was digging at the pile of leaves. That's how I found her body." Lou swallowed. "Though, Detective Cranky thinks I put her there."

Noah's eyebrows jumped. "What?" He craned his neck, noticing that Easton wasn't on the scene. "Oh, it's Roy." The way Noah's normally smooth, cheerful tone flattened at the detective's name told Lou she wasn't the only one who found the man insufferable. "He thinks you could've had something to do with this?" Noah asked.

Lou nodded. "I came to bring Nina an apology basket because she was at the shop yesterday, and Sapphire scratched her."

Noah's chin jutted back. "Sapphy?" Lou appreciated how shocked he was about the news. After all, his young daughter, Marigold, was around Sapphire all the time, and she'd never gotten so much as a swat from the cat. "Even with Maddy's sign?" he asked.

Lou nodded. A sign with tips to wake up a deaf cat had been a suggestion Lou's niece, Maddy, had made after she'd visited that summer. Even as a child, Maddy had understood Sapphire's needs as a deaf cat better than most adults.

"Did she startle him?" Noah asked.

"I think that must've been what happened." Lou felt the stress drain from her body as her friend confirmed not only her cat's good character but also the unreasonableness of Nina's refusal to heed the warning sign Lou had posted about her special cat. "And she threatened to have Sapphy euthanized, as well as file a complaint with the county."

Lou had to admit, now that she repeated it aloud, it wasn't a bad motive for murder. If Detective Anderson thought she was capable of this even before hearing about that detail, he would see her as his top suspect after he learned that fact.

Sapphire was the only thing she had left from her life back in New York City with her late husband, Ben. She also loved the little guy more than anything and would jump in front of a moving car to keep him safe. But she, and anyone who knew her well, had to believe that she wouldn't ever do something like this.

Confirming her hopes, Noah tsked and said, "That's ridiculous. He'll realize the truth the moment he talks to anyone in town. I wouldn't worry about it."

Lou's mouth tugged into a half smile. "Okay, well, if we're not worrying about that, the next thing we need to worry about is finding this little guy a foster home since his person is gone."

Noah turned his attention to the dog. "I'm afraid that's going to be a harder job." He scratched Mr. Muffins on the head. "This little guy, while adorable, has the only case of canine irritable bowel syndrome I've ever encountered. He must be let out every couple of hours, even at night."

Lou thought about the pajamas Nina was wearing. Someone had obviously killed her in the middle of the night, probably on one of those very bathroom outings with Mr. Muffins.

Noah held out his arms. "But I can keep him at the clinic for a few days while we search. Sometimes people are excited to take on an animal with special needs. He's incredibly sweet, so that will help his case."

"Thank you," Lou said, passing the dog to Noah. "I would take him, but I can't commit to letting a dog out that often when I'm the only one working in the bookshop."

"Totally understandable," Noah said, tucking the Pomeranian under his arm. "We'll find someone who can. I'm going to tell Roy that I'm taking him."

Lou stiffened at his mention of the detective. Mr. Muffins didn't seem to be on Detective Anderson's list of concerns at the moment, but she worried he might suddenly fabricate a reason Noah couldn't take the dog.

Showing none of Lou's hesitation, Noah strode right over to Detective Anderson. The pairing of the large, burly man holding the tiny, fluffy dog would've made Lou grin had she not been so worried. Instead of sticking out his chest and scowling down, as the detective had with Lou, his eyes widened in surprise, and he took a step back as he noticed Noah approaching. Detective Anderson had to look up to Noah a little, so he couldn't use his height as an intimidation factor as he had with Lou.

"I'm taking Mr. Muffins. I'll have him at my clinic. Let me know if Nina's got anything in her will about the dog, and we can follow her wishes. If not, I can work on finding him a home." Noah glanced over his shoulder at Lou. "I'm also going to be taking Lou with me. If you need to ask her any more questions, you know where her bookshop is."

Unlike the almost predatory way Detective Anderson had examined Lou when she'd said she was leaving, the man nodded in response to Noah's statement, his eyes flicking to the ground.

Lou's shoulders relaxed. Noah seemed to intimidate the detective. It was funny because Noah was so gentle and kind. She never thought of him as intimidating, but she wasn't mad that he had that effect on Detective Anderson.

"Thank you," she whispered as he walked back to her.

Noah gestured to her car. He got into the passenger side. "I'll ride with you, so he doesn't give you a hard time. Would you drop me off at my place up here? It's the gray one on the right."

Lou complied, noticing the neat little home. She'd never seen Noah's place before. But his truck was parked out front.

"What kind of magic did you work to get him to listen to you?" Lou asked as she pulled to a stop in front of Noah's house. "He treated me like a child. A murderous one."

Noah exhaled a laugh. "Not sure about magic, but his dog got into some chocolate last year, and I saved its life. Roy's treated me with more respect ever since."

Lou made a note of that. Not that she could save a dog's life like Noah could, but maybe she could find ways to be helpful to the detective to earn better treatment as well. "Thank you so much for coming to help."

"Anytime." Noah gave Lou a salute and got out of the car with Mr. Muffins.

Lou knew she could drive home, but she didn't feel right going about her day normally after what she'd seen. Being in the calming presence of Noah made her want more company.

So, instead of going back home, Lou drove to her best friend's house. Normally, Willow would be at the local high school, at work, but she hadn't returned to teaching that fall.

Lou's teenage nieces had visited that summer, and besides helping Lou solve a local mystery, they'd also helped inspire Willow to follow her heart. That had led to two revelations in Willow's life. The first being that she'd finally kissed her neighbor, Detective Easton West, who'd had feelings for her for many years, and she'd realized she shared those feelings. The second revelation had been that, while she loved teaching high schoolers about plants and how to grow them, it was finally time to make her dreams of running her own nursery a reality.

So, Willow was using the fall and winter months to find a location for her business and get things set up for a spring opening.

Lou pulled into Willow's driveway. Instead of walking up to Willow's front door, Lou circumvented the house, and walked around to Willow's lush garden, heading toward the barn where she kept her horse, OC, and pygmy goat, Steve. Willow spent a lot of her time with those two, and it was always where Lou checked first when she came over. But before Lou had gotten even a few yards toward the barn, a whistle caught her attention. She turned to see Willow hanging out of her open sliding glass door.

Turning back toward the house, Lou entered her friend's cozy living room. The scent of cinnamon and cloves sat heavy in the air like a warm blanket, and Lou shivered off the lingering chill from the day's events.

"Hey," Willow said. "To what do I owe this surprise Lou sighting?"

Lou appraised the kitchen table that was completely covered in papers. There were scribbled drawings of different nursery layouts, real estate listings Willow had printed out, spreadsheets full of numbers and totals, and dozens of seed packets. There was also a holiday-scented candle burning in the middle of the table. Willow must've been spending her afternoon on business planning.

Lou sank into her usual spot on Willow's couch. "I've had an interesting twenty-four hours, and I needed to see a friendly face."

"Spill," Willow said, getting Lou a glass of water before settling next to her on the sofa.

Lou told Willow all about Nina's visit to the bookshop the day before, Sapphire's uncharacteristically violent streak, and the apology today that took a turn when Lou found Nina's body in the leaves.

Willow listened intently, frowning, gasping, and clenching her fists in anger at all the right places.

"Ugh. Roy." Willow rolled her eyes as Lou finished explaining how he'd treated her. "Easton hates that guy." Willow sat back and puffed out her cheeks. "Roy's on your case because, believe it or not, there's an even bigger one already taking up Easton's time."

Lou leaned forward.

Willow stood from the couch and paced through the living room, stopping to check the leaves on one of her indoor plants. Even as the leaves were turning outside, Willow's living room was as green as the middle of spring. Indoor plants of every variety sat or hung from every available surface, making Lou feel like she was in a peaceful garden.

Any feeling of peace flew out the window with what Willow said next. "Someone shot Judge Potts early this morning. Easton and I were supposed to have dinner together tonight, but he canceled."

The name of the judge didn't ring a bell, but Lou's mind returned to the pajamas Nina had been wearing when she'd died. It seemed she and Judge Potts could've died around the same time.

"That's awful," Lou said. Despite the bad news, she felt a hint of happiness. "Wait." Lou swiveled her body, throwing an arm over the back of the couch as she followed Willow with her gaze. "Did you say Easton was supposed to take you to dinner?"

The two longtime neighbors had gone on their first official date the week before, and it had gone well, from Willow's reports. While they'd first kissed during the summer at one of Willow's dressage competitions with OC, they'd both been swamped with work and hadn't gotten around to going on an official date for a couple of months.

Willow's cheeks turned pink. "Yeah, we had planned to go to the bistro, but that's okay. I know he has to focus on the case."

Lou's shoulders sank forward. "So I'm stuck with Detective Anderson? I think I'll have to keep Noah around just in case he comes back."

"Noah?" Willow asked, pausing by the table to straighten a pile of papers.

"He was the only person the grumpy detective seemed intimidated by," Lou explained.

"Well, if Noah's not available, I can come give Roy a piece of my mind. Don't worry. You'll be cleared before you know it," Willow reassured her.

Lou sure hoped her friend was right. But there was a terrible pit in her stomach that warned her it might not be that easy.

CHAPTER 4

Lou stayed at Willow's for the rest of the afternoon, helping her with nursery planning and her barn chores. Willow was currently searching for the perfect property in town to house her nursery, and they'd browsed through a few promising prospects. Putting her mind to work on different tasks had helped Lou's worries subside about Nina's murder and Detective Anderson's insistence she was at fault.

She'd just gotten home that evening and was settling into her cozy living room when her phone buzzed with an incoming text message.

> I know you didn't kill Nina.

Lou's lips parted in shock. She clicked on her screen, checking to see who'd sent the message, but it was connected to a random phone number she didn't recognize.

> Who is this?

There was no answer. Waiting felt so anticlimactic after the excitement and fear that had washed over her upon receiving the text.

Lou paced through her apartment for almost thirty minutes. The cats paced with her, darting around her feet and watching her like they were expecting something to happen. But no other text came in response.

"Let's try a different tactic," she said to the cats.

How do you know?

An answer came through almost immediately.

I think I know who actually killed her.

Lou's entire body flushed hot and then cold. What? Her fingers flew over the phone screen as she typed a response.

Why are you talking to me, then? Tell the police.

No response came through, and Lou wondered if she'd possibly asked another question they were unwilling to answer, but then her phone vibrated with a response.

Can't.

That was it.

She chewed on her lip. Why? seemed like the obvious response to that one-word answer. But she also figured that if they were going to tell her, they would've already elaborated. She wasn't sure why, but she didn't want to scare them away.

Before she could think of what else to say, they added another text.

> You solve mysteries around here, right? Help me solve this one.

Around here. So, it was someone in Button. And it was someone who knew things about her. An icy feeling settled on the back of her neck and tingled down her spine. This mystery texter knew a lot about her, it seemed, yet she knew nothing about them. First of all, how had they gotten her cell phone number? Her website for the bookshop listed the shop phone, not her personal number. Second, they knew she was a suspect in Nina's murder. Had they been at the scene?

While those questions felt important, Lou needed to find out the most crucial information first.

Inhaling, she typed a response.

> Why do you only *think* you know who the killer is? Why aren't you sure?

> Sometimes I can't trust my eyes … or my brain.

Lou contemplated the confusing sentence. Why? Again, asking them seemed futile, since they hadn't elaborated on anything so far.

Pulling up her text thread with Willow, Lou took a screenshot of the conversation with the mystery person and sent it to her friend. She thought about sending it to Easton, but Willow had mentioned that he was swamped with the judge case, and Lou felt better about running it by her friend first.

> Just got this odd text. What should I do?

Lou added the picture after her message. Willow responded right away.

Um ... weird. Let me see if Easton's available.

Lou tapped her fingers on her phone case while she waited.

He's not answering. Sorry. I would take it to Roy if I were you. Unfortunately.

Lou sighed.

Okay, that's what I was thinking too. Thanks.

Do you want me to come with?

Thanks for the offer, but I'll see how it goes on my own. Maybe he'll be happy about the potential for clues.

Lou's thoughts returned to Noah's story about helping the detective's dog. Maybe this could be her olive branch. Maybe this could be the piece that changed Detective Anderson's opinion of her.

Willow sent back a thumbs-up.

As much as Lou wanted to stay in and enjoy a fire on a cozy fall evening, she got her purse, put her jacket back on, and ventured out into the darkening evening.

The police station was only a few blocks down from the bookshop, so Lou didn't bother with the car. The smoky scent of fires crackling away in people's fireplaces all throughout town mixed perfectly with the fresh, cold air, putting Lou in a better mood for her walk.

Her good mood only intensified when she entered the police

station to find the front desk empty. Officer Reynolds, a crotchety man, typically sat behind the desk, so Lou wasn't sad to see it unmanned.

She bypassed the front desk and wandered down the hallway where Easton's office was located, assuming the two detectives would work in the same area. Easton's office was dark, but light spilled out of the one next to his. The door was open, and the nameplate read *Dt. Anderson*.

Lou couldn't believe she hadn't noticed that before. She considered herself to be a very detail-oriented person, but she was clearly losing her edge if a second detective had worked in town this whole time, and she'd completely missed him.

Knocking on the doorframe, Lou peered into the office. Detective Anderson sat behind his desk, glowering at a folder. He looked up, refocusing his glare at her.

"Hi." Lou stepped inside the office. "Something weird happened. I thought you might want to see it." She pulled out her phone and brought up the conversation with the mystery texter. Turning the device toward him, she slid it across the desk.

The detective's eyes skimmed over the screen, staring at the texts for a few seconds as he moved the screen up with his finger to read them all. Setting down the phone, he trained his gaze on her again. "Do you mind if I take a picture of your screen?"

She shook her head. "Please do."

After snapping pictures of the conversation, Detective Anderson turned to his laptop and typed something. The clacking of keys rang through the otherwise silent room. Excitement built in Lou. This might be it. She'd brought something helpful to the detective, so maybe he would treat her with more respect now.

Detective Anderson stopped typing, staring at the laptop screen as he read through the results of whatever he had searched. After a quick narrowing of his eyes, he looked back at her.

"Nice try." He let out a dry laugh.

Lou blinked at him, not sure what to say. "I'm sorry. What?"

Okay … so maybe this was not her chance to earn his respect.

He pointed at the phone. "That's an unregistered number. It's a burner phone."

Lou waited.

"This is probably you. You could've easily bought a phone and texted yourself to make it seem like you're innocent," Roy scoffed. "I'm not falling for it."

"Falling for what?" Any hope Lou had of getting help from the police left her in a huff.

He cocked an eyebrow. "If I can get a location triangulation on this number, I'd bet anything it's going to come up somewhere in Button. Don't you think? You could've at least driven to a different town to text yourself."

Lou let out a frustrated sigh. "You're not going to take this seriously?"

"Oh, I'm taking it seriously. I'm adding it to your file." He cleared his throat. "*The* file." The smirk he wore told Lou he'd meant to make that slip.

Disappointment swirled around Lou. She stood and grabbed her phone off his desk. She didn't say anything as she turned on her heel and stormed out the door. Stomping her way home vented the worst of her anger, which was a good thing because Willow called just as she entered the bookshop and locked the door behind her.

"Hey," Lou answered, biting out the word.

"Whoa." Willow let out a whistle. "I'm guessing the talk with Roy didn't go well?"

"Nope. He thinks I bought a burner phone and texted myself to appear innocent."

Willow was silent for a beat. "Actually, that wouldn't be a terrible idea."

Lou groaned.

"Sorry," Willow said. "Well, I talked to Easton and showed him the convo, but I don't think you're going to like what he had to say either."

"He thinks I'm a murderer too?" Lou asked sarcastically, stopping in the middle of the bookshop.

"Of course not." Willow laughed like that was the craziest thing Lou had ever said. "But he thinks your texter might be."

Lou's heart raced. Wait. The murderer might be the person messaging her? Why hadn't she even considered that?

"Easton says that the fact that they're spying on you means they could've been monitoring the scene. Killers often do that," Willow explained.

"You don't say?" Lou's tone was flat as she remembered Detective Anderson's earlier comment about just that characteristic.

"Yeah," Willow said, missing Lou's sarcasm. "And he thinks they might've seen you asking questions and got worried you might know too much. Lou, they might be trying to get you out of the equation."

The room seemed to tilt around Lou. She placed her hand on a bookshelf to steady herself. "So I shouldn't text the person anymore?" Lou asked as the realization sank in.

"Easton didn't think it would be a good idea." Willow's tone dropped with concern. "And I agree with him."

That was enough for Lou. She and Willow had been best

friends practically their entire lives. She trusted her friend to always have her best interests at heart.

"I do too," Lou said. "I don't know why I hadn't considered it being the murderer, but he's right. The risk is too high. I think I just got excited that someone believed me after talking to Detective Anderson and having him treat me like I was a murderer."

"Totally understandable. But the best thing you can do at this point is stay as far away from this investigation as you can," Willow said.

"Did you and Easton get to have dinner after all?" Lou asked. "Or did you just talk to him via text?"

"Text, unfortunately," Willow said. "But I can't fault him for being busy. I'm busy too. Oh, I forgot to tell you. I think I found the perfect spot for the nursery."

"Yeah?" Lou sank into the couch in the middle of the bookstore. She didn't have the mental energy to head upstairs to her apartment just yet. "Is it one of the properties we looked through today?"

"Actually, no," Willow's tone exuded excitement. "Cassidy called me a few minutes ago with an idea, and I kind of love it. It's that abandoned parking lot on the corner of Needle Street and Ribbon Road, where that traveling carnival set up just a couple of weeks ago."

"Oh," Lou said. "That is an excellent location." Earlier, when they were searching through listings together, they'd been trying to find the perfect combination of space, a fair price, and accessibility. None of the properties they'd found had all three qualities. "And it's okay that it's paved?" Lou asked. Most of the places Willow had considered so far were not.

"It's preferable, believe it or not. Easier for people's carts to move around, and it won't get muddy when I water all the time," Willow explained. "Plus, most nurseries don't grow on the same land where they sell. It's also dirt cheap, which will help toward renting land for the growing part of the operation."

"I'm so happy for you, Willow." Lou scrunched up her shoulders. "Let me know how I can help."

"I will. We've gotta keep you busy so you're not tempted to get yourself involved in this murder investigation." Willow chuckled.

Lou did too. And honestly, she really thought she wouldn't have a hard time staying far away from Nina's death. Little did she know how swiftly things would change.

CHAPTER 5

The next day was more than enough to keep Lou's mind off Nina's death and the mysterious texts she'd received.

Forrest, one of her regulars, walked into the bookshop that morning as usual. But instead of holding his normal latte, his large hands were cupped around a white cat. Well, white wasn't exactly how Lou would describe the cat. While it shared the same striking blue eyes as Sapphire, this cat was almost a cream color with accents of orange on its nose, along its back and tail, and on each of its legs.

"And who's this?" Lou asked, holding out her hands to take the cat from Forrest.

She knew it was for her because, even though Forrest loved cats, his wife was allergic and couldn't live with one; hence, Forrest coming to the bookshop daily to get his cat fix.

"Gianna actually found the little one hiding under her car this morning, trying to stay dry," Forrest explained. "I would've taken it to Noah myself, but the clinic isn't open yet, and I have an early client." He pointed toward his office, where he held therapy sessions.

"Don't worry," Lou said. "I've got it from here. Thank you so much."

Forrest left for his appointment, promising to be back later. He slipped out the door just as Lou's other regulars filed inside. A misty rain fell from the sky, almost like a wet fog, causing people to squint and hunch over as they walked through it.

Silas peeled out of his jacket, waved hello to Lou, and settled into his normal spot. While Silas had a heart for all cats, his true love was Catnip Everdeen, a normally shy cat who loved Silas above all others. The old man removed his bowler hat and patted his lap. Catnip jumped right up and curled into a contented ball.

George, a twentysomething tech genius, headed straight for Lou's newest arrival. "So pretty. Did I see Forrest drop it off and run?" she asked.

Lou scratched the kitten's head. "Yeah. He has an early client. Would you watch the shop for a second while I take this little one to the back room and make sure it's separated from the other cats?"

George said she would, and Lou took the proper precautions to make sure the new cat was comfortable but removed. She'd made the mistake of introducing a new cat before Noah had the chance to do a wellness check and ended up with a bookstore full of flea-ridden felines. So, Lou set the new cat up in a crate with a cozy towel, water, and food. The little thing was eating and purring contentedly when she left it.

George was squinting at her phone when Lou walked back to the bookshop register.

"It's a flame-point Siamese," she explained, showing Lou a picture of a cream-colored cat just like their newest arrival.

Lou nodded, impressed. "I've never heard of such a thing, but it's beautiful."

The doorbell jangled, and in walked Noah.

"That was fast," George said.

Noah's eyebrows lifted in question. He looked at Lou.

"I didn't even text him yet," she said.

Noah slid his hands into his pockets. "I was coming to check on you after yesterday. Is there something else you need me for?" He assessed the bookshop, scanning for something that might be leaking or broken.

In addition to keeping everyone's pets healthy and happy, Noah was a handyman. The list of things she could need his help with was long.

"Forrest just brought in a cat. Gianna found it hiding under her car this morning. I just came back from setting it up in the back room with food and water." Lou gestured to the back room.

"You two go ahead." George waved them back. "I've got things covered up here."

Lou and Noah made their way to the bookshop's office that doubled as Lou's cat headquarters. It was where she kept their litter boxes, food, and their travel crates. She gestured to the cozy crate she'd just set up for the little stray.

"A flame point," Noah said as he pulled the cat from the crate Lou had put it in. "Gorgeous."

Lou agreed. "I've never seen anything like it before."

"Him," Noah said, continuing his examination. He turned his attention to Lou. "You can think of his name while I take him back to the clinic with me and see if he's microchipped and caught up on his shots."

"Oh, I don't need any time." Lou crossed her arms smugly. "I'd say this guy is a Holden Clawfield, for sure." She'd thought of that name the other day and had been dying to use it.

Noah gave her a dimpled grin, showing he approved.

"How's Mr. Muffins?" Lou asked as Noah put Holden back in the crate to prepare for his trip to the clinic.

"Good." Noah's expression softened even further. "I had him at my place last night, but Kathleen said she'll take him for a stint. She doesn't mind letting him out in the middle of the night. Says she doesn't get more than a few hours sleep at a time as it is."

Kathleen was Noah's clinic manager, and besides running the clinic seamlessly, she had a heart for animals and people alike.

"I'll see you soon, Holden," Lou called after the cat as Noah tucked the cat carrier under his arm, and Lou went to relieve George.

THE SHOP WAS SLOW the rest of the morning, which wasn't odd for a Tuesday. But between the sleepy pace and the drizzly weather, Lou was really looking forward to closing up at lunch and snuggling upstairs with a good book. About a half hour before she closed, Forrest showed up.

"How's the kitten?" He scanned the shop as if he expected to see it.

"He's great. With Noah right now." Lou smiled.

Forrest nodded. "Well, I know you're about to close up. I just wanted to stop and check on the little fellow."

"Holden Clawfield," Lou corrected him.

Forrest let out a deep chuckle. "Perfect. See you tomorrow, Lou."

She locked the door behind him and padded upstairs with the cats to have lunch and curl up with a book by the window so she could watch the rain.

But just as she finished lunch, she got a text from Willow.

Whatcha doing?

Depends. I might have a new cat, but he's with Noah right now. I'm not sure if he's bringing him back today. Let me text him and see.

Lou checked in with Noah.

How's Holden Clawfield doing?

Great!

Noah sent the response right away. He followed it up with,

He doesn't have a microchip and isn't on any of the missing pet message boards. He also wasn't neutered, so I took care of that. Because of the surgery, I want to keep him overnight for observation, if that's okay.

Perfect. Thank you!

Lou sent back. Then, to Willow, she sent,

I'm free. Cat isn't coming here until tomorrow. What are you thinking? Need help with nursery stuff?

I was thinking we could do some leaf peeping. I heard the foliage a little north of us is gorgeous near the river.

Excitement built in Lou. She was a total leaf peeper. Back in

New York, she and Ben used to drive up to Vermont and see the beautiful fall colors.

I'm in! Want me to drive?

Nah, I'll come pick you up. See you in a few.

Lou had just changed into her cozy boots and added a warm scarf to the cable-knit sweater she'd been wearing, when Willow pulled up in front of the bookstore. Lou hopped in and was met with the scent of roasted coffee and brown sugar.

"I made us lattes." Willow beamed.

Lou buckled herself in and wrapped her fingers around the travel mug, savoring the smell of the drink. "Thank you. I think you read my autumn wish-list diary."

Willow chuckled. "I don't think I needed to, since I'm pretty sure our wish lists are the same." As she pulled away from the curb, Willow explained how she and Cassidy had toured the lot on the corner of Needle Street and Ribbon Road.

"Is it the place?" Lou asked, her shoulders rose with anticipation.

Willow's eyes sparkled with excitement. "I think it's too perfect to pass up."

Lou let her shoulders drop with an exhale. "That's wonderful. I'm so happy for you."

She pushed past the memories of the traveling carnival that had stopped there a couple of weeks ago, glad Willow's nursery would take over the space and fill it with better memories.

Willow drove north. As she did, they chatted about Lou's newest foster.

The scenery was breathtaking. Northeast of Button was a rather large city, but Willow strayed Northwest, turning toward the Skagit River where farmland took over the valley landscape. That was where they found some of the most vibrant colors. Trees dipped golden leaves down toward the road, curving in a colorful canopy over Willow's car. Stark reds and flaming oranges accented the golden base of oak trees along the back roads. Crunchy dried leaves that had already fallen whirled around in the air currents behind the car as it sped by.

They pulled off the road in a few places to ooh and ahh at the colors, pointing out wildlife to each other as it hopped, bounded, or flew by. Lou sipped at her coffee, cozy in Willow's car, happy as could be. But when she glanced over at her friend, she noticed Willow's fingers were clenched tight around the steering wheel, and she wasn't pulling back onto the road after their latest stop.

"Is everything okay?" Lou asked, setting down her coffee.

Willow let her hands drop into her lap. "Yeah, I was just thinking about that property for the nursery."

"I thought you said it was perfect." Lou shifted her weight in her seat.

"It is," Willow agreed. "There's just one catch." She squinted one eye.

"What's that?" Lou frowned at her friend.

Willow scratched at her forehead. "If I go with this property, it means I'm definitely going to have to rent out land on which to grow everything, since I can do some things in the greenhouses, but I'll need soil and light to grow the variety of plants I've dreamed of offering."

Lou hadn't visited many nurseries over the years, especially living in a big city for the past couple of decades. She hadn't had room for much more than a few indoor plants. But she trusted that if Willow said she needed land to make her nursery work, it was a necessity.

"What are you going to do?" Lou asked. "Could you grow on your property?"

Willow's property, while a few acres, was mostly taken up by her barn, the paddocks, and a regulation-sized arena that helped her practice for the dressage competitions she and OC often entered during the summer months. But maybe she would sacrifice some of that space for her nursery.

"I have an even better idea." Willow cleared her throat. Her attention shifted to the driveway just beyond where she'd pulled off the road. Lou followed her gaze. The mailbox was a cute little red barn with the name Milton painted on the side.

"This stop wasn't just to look at that grouping of maples," Lou said as the realization hit her. She turned back to Willow. "You pulled over here for a reason. Didn't you?"

Willow chewed on her lip. "I may have brought you out here under false pretenses."

CHAPTER 6

Lou leaned back in her seat and shuffled her feet in discomfort. She would do anything for Willow, and her friend knew that. If she'd told her what she really wanted to do, Lou would've followed her, no matter what.

"Why the secrecy?" Lou asked warily.

Willow sighed. "This is Milton Farm. Until about five years ago, this farm was a major producer of plants for local nurseries. In fact, the nurseries that were in Button and Brine went out of business after Milton Farm stopped selling plants to them, unable to charge the higher prices needed to source from the bigger companies in the Pacific Northwest like Silver Lake Nursery does," Willow explained.

"Why'd they stop selling?" Lou asked, peering out at the land. It was overgrown and looked more like a wild landscape than a working farm.

"Benji Milton passed away." Willow bowed her head slightly. "His wife, Peggy Lee, shut down. She wasn't very sociable to begin with, but once she lost Benji, she isolated herself completely."

The farmland seemed to morph before Lou's eyes as Willow told the story of the people who lived there. Where she'd seen a wild landscape, at first, she now saw greenhouses that had become overcome by the surrounding plants. Most of all, she saw a life that had been forgotten after a substantial loss. Her heart hurt.

Willow gazed at the scraggly land in the same way she admired OC, her beloved horse, like he was the greatest thing in this world. "I wasn't even sure what shape it would be in, honestly. But this is perfect."

"Perfect?" Lou asked, blinking in surprise.

There were a lot of words to describe the farm in front of her, but perfect would not be on Lou's list.

Willow rubbed her hands together. "See how overgrown it is? That means the soil's still nutritious. I was worried it would be all dried up and tilled out. I wasn't sure what she'd done with the place. It looks like she hasn't done a thing." Willow pulled the car forward, heading down the long driveway.

"And you didn't want to get your hopes up," Lou said, understanding why her friend had kept their stop here a secret until now.

Willow nodded. She believed in intention and wouldn't want to jinx the fact that she'd found the perfect place for her nursery by assuming she had also found a farm on which to grow the plants she would sell. They bumped along the pothole-riddled drive as the farmhouse grew slowly nearer.

Lou swallowed. "And you're going to ask Peggy Lee to start up a business again? To grow and sell to you?"

"No," Willow said. "I don't think she'd do that. Benji was the real green thumb behind their operation. My proposal takes nothing on her end. I just want to rent the land from her and use it to grow and harvest for my nursery."

Lou thought it sounded like a good idea. "Do you want me to come with?" she asked when Willow came to a stop and put the car in park.

Willow shook her head, surveying the farmhouse. Weathered as it was, it was still beautiful. The place had a 360-degree wraparound porch, black shutters, and a shiny red front door. Despite peeling in a few places, the white paint on the siding was holding up well.

"I want to talk to her alone the first time, if you don't mind," Willow said.

Lou understood. This was Willow's dream, and she wanted to do the legwork.

Willow pulled in a deep breath and got out of the car. She glanced over her shoulder as she approached the front porch. Lou gave her a thumbs-up through the windshield, and Willow walked up the rest of the way. Lou lost sight of her as she went up to the door, but she saw Willow again less than a minute later when she ran back down the porch.

An onion and two small peppers came flying after Willow. She ducked and tore back to the car, panting as she slipped back inside. A carrot hit the windshield.

"What happened?" Lou asked, eyes wide.

"I knocked on the door." Willow's chest rose and fell as she caught her breath. "And I had only just introduced myself when she started throwing vegetables at me."

Lou gawked at the porch in disbelief. "You weren't kidding when you said she's antisocial."

Willow leaned closer to the windshield to inspect the carrot. "At least we know the soil's still great." She pointed to the vegetable. "If she grew that herself, which I'd bet she did, it looks lovely."

Lou had to point out the obvious. "But it doesn't seem like that's going to help you, if she won't even talk to you."

"Right." Willow clicked her tongue. "Oh well. Shall we head home?"

Lou nodded. Twenty minutes later, the two friends pulled back into Button in quiet defeat.

The quiet hadn't been immediate. At first, after she'd climbed into the car after being chased off by Peggy Lee, Willow had verbally processed what had happened, assuring Lou that she didn't need Milton Farm and would find another place that was even better. By the seventh repetition, Lou realized Willow was trying to convince herself.

That was when the silence had fallen over the car.

Lou didn't know what to say. Well, she knew what she *could* say. She knew she could reassure Willow that she would find something better. She also knew Willow would see right through her lie. Instead of making empty promises or telling her friend lies, Lou vowed to keep working to make this part of Willow's dream a reality.

But as Willow pulled up in front of the bookstore to drop Lou off that evening, Lou's thoughts tunneled into one thing and one thing only.

Because parked next to them was Detective Roy Anderson and a team of four officers. From the way they were climbing out of the sedan as Willow parked, it appeared they had just arrived. Or maybe they'd been waiting for Lou to get home.

A pit of dread formed in the bottom of Lou's stomach. In her fear, Lou forgot Willow was in the car with her until her friend reached out and grabbed her hand, squeezing tight. Keeping with the silence that had formed during the last part of their drive, Willow said nothing. Like Lou, she didn't make any empty promises. Her blue eyes locked on to Lou's with the same silent promise Lou had just made to Willow.

I am here for you. I will do everything in my power to make sure you are okay.

With a single nod to tell Willow that she believed her, Lou unbuckled her seat belt and slipped out of the car. Detective Anderson stepped forward, his team waiting behind him in the shadows, closer to the bookstore. He held a piece of paper in his hand and wore a smug smile Lou had no problem seeing, even in the dark. Willow stepped up next to Lou as the detective held the paper forward. She snapped it out of his hand before Lou even had the wherewithal to reach forward.

"A search warrant?" Willow scoffed. "For a leash?"

Detective Anderson cocked an eyebrow. "A thin, bright-blue leash. The medical examiner believes that to be the murder weapon, and it was most likely wielded by a person of average height, much like yourself, Mrs. Henry. Smaller people often use things to strangle people because their hands aren't big or powerful enough to wrap around a person's throat. We have multiple witnesses who've seen such a leash in Mrs. Henry's establishment."

Lou's eyes widened with recognition. She *had* bought a leash for Sapphire on their trip across the country. She'd put it on him when she'd had to take him out of his cat carrier in the airport, but she hadn't used it since.

"I don't even know where that is," she said, surprising herself. She usually knew details like that. This case, and her involvement as a suspect, was really throwing her off.

"I'll be the judge of that," Detective Anderson said. "In addition to seeing the leash here. Multiple witnesses saw the victim threaten to euthanize your cat, heard your statement about not letting that woman hurt him, and we found a complaint filed with the county, sitting on the victim's counter." He lifted his chin. Unlike with Lou, he couldn't use his height against Willow since she stood just as tall as him.

As Lou listened to the detective, she got the distinct impression that he didn't have to share the information, and maybe even shouldn't be telling her everything. He was *happy* to share it. He reveled in Lou knowing the list of things he had on her.

Lou gestured to the bookshop. "You didn't need a search warrant. I would've let you look through my house and bookshop if you'd asked. I have nothing to hide."

Willow shoved the paper back toward the detective and wrapped a supportive arm around Lou's shoulders. "That's right," she said.

It started to mist again, something for which Lou was very grateful. The bad weather meant there were fewer people out walking through downtown Button to see the police searching Lou's bookshop and apartment, or to see Detective Anderson leave with a blue leash in an evidence bag a short while later.

After assuring Willow she was just fine, and sending Willow home, Lou tidied her home robotically. She couldn't seem to comprehend that the police had just been here, combing through her things for evidence that they hoped would prove that she had strangled that woman.

It was so absurd, Lou almost wanted to laugh. It was also very real and scary, and it made Lou want to cry just as much.

She'd seen enough true crime shows to know that innocent people could go to prison for crimes they didn't commit. Just because she knew she hadn't killed Nina didn't mean Detective Anderson wouldn't do everything in his power to put her behind bars for the crime.

Fear bubbled up inside her, taking over. She flipped her phone in her hands, her thoughts turning over and over with the device.

Then, without thinking too hard, Lou unlocked the screen and pulled up her text-message threads. She opened the one from the mystery texter. She'd kept telling herself that she would delete the thread and block the number but hadn't done it yet. Each time she'd gone to do so, her fingers froze, unable to execute the command her rational brain was giving.

The last text the mystery person had sent sat at the bottom of the screen like a pit in the bottom of Lou's stomach.

> Sometimes I can't trust my eyes ... or my brain.

The mystery texter knew something. They'd seen something. They just didn't have all the pieces of the puzzle.

In her desperation, Lou created a story in her mind that it couldn't be the killer. This humble, unsure person couldn't be the one to strangle Nina. If they had, why would they reach out to Lou? No, this was someone like Lou, who'd been in the wrong place at the wrong time.

Before she changed her mind, she texted them back.

> Okay. Where do I start?

She sucked in a breath as she pressed send, feeling as if she'd set something in motion that she couldn't take back.

A reply came back almost immediately.

> The neighbors.

A flush of worry raced through Lou, but she shoved the

feeling aside. The mystery texter believed she was innocent. That was more than she could say for Detective Anderson.

CHAPTER 7

It was a good thing that the following day was Wednesday because if it had been a Monday or Tuesday, Lou would've been tempted to close the bookshop, drive over to Nina's house, and start questioning her neighbors immediately. Wednesdays were usually quite busy, and that day was no exception.

A steady stream of customers didn't stop her from continually checking her phone, rereading the text, and contemplating what it meant. The neighbors. Did that mean one of Nina's neighbors was the killer, or did one of her neighbors know something helpful? As tempted as she was to ask, the shop kept her busy enough that she never had a long enough span of time to decide what exactly to ask the mystery texter.

That didn't mean Lou stopped thinking about it. She was so distracted, her regulars noticed.

"Everything okay?" Forrest asked.

Silas frowned. "Yeah, you keep looking at your phone like you're expecting bad news."

Lou sent them her most reassuring smile. "I'm just trying to figure out a puzzle."

The men went back to their reading, as if they knew they wouldn't get more information out of her, much like she'd instinctively known certain questions wouldn't garner an answer from the mystery texter.

Noah came in around lunchtime, toting a cat carrier. Holden Clawfield peered out from behind the metal door.

"He's all caught up on his vaccinations, and he's officially off the market for making little Holdens." Noah chuckled. "He's still healing, so make sure he's not too active for the next few days. We did a flea treatment before his surgery, so he should be okay to join the other cats now. Just check him with a comb for a couple of days."

Lou nodded. Ever since *fleapocalypse*, as she'd dubbed the last outbreak, she checked the cats regularly to stay on top of the pests.

"Thank you so much for doing all that." Lou rocked back on her heels. "I don't know what we would do without you."

Noah waved a hand toward her. "It's been oddly slow at the clinic this week, so I'm taking advantage of it." He watched as Lou extracted Holden from the crate and let him down in the middle of the bookshop.

There weren't any customers at the moment, and Lou wanted to take advantage of the lull so that she could focus on how Holden would get along with the other cats. She and Noah watched as he stretched and tentatively walked forward. Sapphire was fast asleep in a warm beam of fall sunshine coming through the front window of the shop, but Anne Mice and Catnip Everdeen slunk over, touching noses with Holden Clawfield in a feline hello. After that interaction, they seemed comfortable enough with each other, and the two female cats wandered in front of Holden like they were giving him a tour.

Seeing they were fine, Noah crossed his arms over his chest and looked over at Lou. "And how are you doing? Any more run-ins with Roy?"

Lou wrinkled her nose. "He stopped by last night with a search warrant." She lifted her hands palms up. "He and a team came through, and they took the leash I used with Sapphire when we traveled across the country."

Concern etched itself into wrinkles on Noah's forehead. "A leash? Why?" Now the concern had spread into his tone.

"Apparently, that's the murder weapon. What the killer used to strangle Nina," Lou explained.

"And he's still convinced you're the one who strangled her?" Noah scratched at his cheek.

Lou sighed. "Nina filed that complaint with the county about my shop and my 'dangerous' cat." Lou gestured to the peacefully sleeping Sapphy. She held out a finger to show him that was only one of many strikes against her. "They found the complaint on her counter and think I got rid of her so that it wouldn't go any further. Then they found blue nylon fibers on Nina's neck, fitting a thin leash, like that of a small dog or cat. Which I had." She extended a second finger. "Oh, and the killer must've been about my size, so they're convinced it's me." She held up a third finger, then let her hand drop in defeat.

"Roy does a lot of catering to the judges in the area," Noah said. "I think it means they humor him sometimes, even when things don't quite add up." He held her gaze with his. "Are you considering getting a lawyer?"

Lou shrugged. "I don't know. Until last night, I was content in knowing that I didn't do this, so how could he possibly find me guilty? But now all I can think about is how often innocent people go to prison for crimes they didn't commit and well ... I'm a little scared."

Noah placed a hand on her shoulder for a second, in support. "I understand. Is there any way I can help?"

"You mean, besides being next to me any time I have to deal with Detective Anderson?" Lou joked.

Noah smiled, his dimple deepening with the action.

"Um, I don't know what I need," Lou answered truthfully after a moment. She chewed on her lip as she thought about the mystery texter. "Actually, there might be one thing."

Noah raised his eyebrows in a way that said *ask away*.

"What can you tell me about your neighborhood?" she asked. "About Nina's immediate neighbors, especially."

"Hmmm." Noah ran a hand along his beard-covered chin, the motion making a scratching noise. "Well, behind her are the Fraziers. On her left is Chase Humphrey. And across the street are the Whelans. Is that what you mean?"

"Yes," Lou said. "Do you know of any who were in conflict with her?" She remembered Chase's comment about how she was a terrible woman, and he wouldn't help her if she were drowning. "Chase Humphrey didn't seem too happy with her."

Noah studied the ceiling while he thought. "You know, our mailman was talking the other day about how Chase is selling his house." Noah shook his head. "But he told me after a long day at the clinic, and I'm sorry to say, I didn't pay close attention to the details."

"That's okay. This gives me a place to start," Lou said. "I figure I should go chat with Chase. You know, if Roy's so convinced it was me, maybe he's not following up on other suspects." She pressed her lips together, not wanting to admit that she was working off a hunch from the mystery texter, who could very well be the killer.

Noah gave her a sidelong glance. She wondered for a moment if he would try to talk her out of it, tell her it was too dangerous.

"Want company?" he asked.

Lou did a double take, surprised by his question. "I would love it, actually. I was going to go over there after I close the shop today."

"Great. I'm done around the same time." Noah narrowed his eyes. "Chase is a pretty private guy. What's your plan to get him to talk?"

Lou didn't have a plan. Yet. "Say we're selling cookies?"

Noah chuckled, but his manner turned contemplative. "Maybe we could use that information about his house possibly going up for sale. We could say you're interested, and Cassidy heard through the grapevine that he might be selling."

Grinning, Lou said, "Noah, you're a genius. That's perfect."

He pushed his broad shoulders back proudly. "I haven't been called a genius in a while." A light-pink color tinted his cheeks and his neck. He cleared his throat. "Okay, why don't you come to my place after work, and we can walk down to Chase's together?"

"Sounds great." Lou waved as Noah headed back to the clinic.

Now, all she had to do was wait.

HOLDEN CLAWFIELD TURNED out to be a great distraction during the rest of the time Lou was open that day. Well, *great* might not be the correct word. *Worrisome* distraction was more like it.

He was super sweet, and so cute, but the little guy had one enormous flaw: each time the door was open, he tried to escape.

With all the foster cats she'd had up to that point, she'd yet to have an escape artist.

And in a retail bookstore, the door opened constantly. Lou hadn't ever given a second thought to the number of times people came and went because the other cats steered clear of the front door for the most part. Catnip Everdeen spent most of the day hiding, unless Silas was there, and Anne Mice seemed mildly scared of the bell on the door, so she gave it a wide berth.

But Holden? The bell became an alert for him, the gunshot at the start of a race. Once he heard the bell, he was a cream-colored streak, shooting across the bookshop, toward the open door.

Lou took to positioning herself by the front door like a defender on a basketball court anytime the bell rang, moving right and left to block the cat as he hurtled toward freedom. She got quite a few confused glances from customers as they entered, but it all seemed to make sense once they saw Holden trying his best to escape.

After ringing up her last sale of the day, Lou preemptively picked up Holden as the final customer grabbed her books and started for the door. Lou followed the woman outside, finishing their conversation. Holden strained against Lou's arms until the moment the cool autumn air hit his fur. Then he relaxed into Lou.

Her heart melted. "You're just an outside kinda guy, aren't you?" she said, scratching his head endearingly. "Well, it looks like we have to find a place where you're going to be happy, then."

He purred for the first time all day. When Lou turned back toward the bookshop, he clawed at her shoulder, as if saying, "No! Don't take me back inside."

Lou laughed. "I promise I'll find you a home where you can

be outside, but for today you need to go back in the shop," she explained.

As if he understood—or maybe he was just tired from bolting all day—he gave up the fight and let her take him back inside. Once he and the other cats had been fed an early dinner, she left for Noah's house.

He was waiting for her at his front door when she pulled up. There was a fleece cat bed tucked under his arm.

"For Holden," he said, motioning to her car.

"Thank you." Lou put the bed in her back seat.

Noah and his nine-year-old daughter, Marigold, had made each of the foster cats their own beds. Noah's family owned Material Girls, the quilt shop in town, and both he and his daughter were skilled sewers.

Once she locked her car, they started walking toward Chase Humphrey's house. Noah went over their plan as they walked.

"I touched base with Cass, and she said he's selling it himself, not involving an agent. That's even better for us. It makes sense that you would come talk to him directly," Noah explained.

"But I need to make sure I stay neutral. I'd hate to get his hopes up when I'm not actually interested." Lou fiddled with the hem of her jacket.

"True," Noah said. "And from what Cassidy heard, he's selling because he can't afford the place anymore, so he really needs the money."

Lou didn't like the sound of that. The inability to afford one's home sounded like a terrible turn of life events.

"He was home in the middle of the day when I came around to bring that basket to Nina on Monday. Maybe he got laid off from his job," Lou hypothesized. "He couldn't be older than fifty, so unless he was incredibly smart with his money, I doubt he's retired yet."

Noah ran a hand through his hair. "I can't help you there. I know my neighbors' names, but I definitely don't know a lot about what they do."

As they approached Chase's sage-green house, Lou noted how there were no leaves in his yard, yet Nina's was full of them. But she'd had a whole pile over her. Lou brought up the disconnect with Noah.

"Wouldn't her yard be cleared if there had been a pile?" she asked as she finished her explanation.

Noah nodded. "I could've sworn I saw two gigantic bags of leaves sitting in front of Chase's house this weekend."

"But anyone could've used those to dump over Nina's body," Lou realized.

"Or they could've been picked up. Our pickup day is Monday morning."

That didn't help them.

Lou knocked on the front door, just as she had the day she found Nina's body. She stepped back and waited.

Chase came to the door a few seconds later. Recognition crossed his features, and then his face crumpled into a suspicious frown.

"Have more baskets to bring my terrible neighbor?" he asked with a snort.

Lou waited a beat to make sure her tone was free of judgment when she said, "Well, no, since that neighbor is dead."

"Not soon enough, if you ask me." He cut his gaze to the left, glaring at Nina's house as if it were an extension of her and she'd be able to feel his anger.

Noah coughed in surprise. Lou shifted her weight in discomfort.

"We're actually here because we heard you might be selling your house. Are you still leaving, now that she's gone?" Lou asked as conversationally as she could manage.

"Yes, unfortunately. I love my house, despite the terrible neighbor." He jabbed a thumb toward Nina's house. "That woman is the reason I have to sell. I can't afford to live here anymore ever since she buried me in legal fees."

CHAPTER 8

"Legal fees?" Lou asked, surprise coating the question.

"Yeah, you didn't hear?" Chase directed that question to Noah, who shook his head. Chase rolled his eyes. "It was the fence."

Lou and Noah leaned back to peer at the space in between Chase and Nina's houses. There was no fence.

"There *used* to be a fence," Chase said, seeing their confusion. "In fact, it was there since before either Nina or I bought our houses." Chase motioned toward the front steps. He shut the door behind him and led them around to the front of the house to his side yard. "And she'd lived there for five years with no issue. But then suddenly, I get a notice from a lawyer that my fence is on her property." Chase stopped and held out his hand, showing them the line where the old fence used to be.

"Was it?" Noah asked.

"Yes. Three feet." Chase let out a cynical snort. "I tried to fight it, since I hadn't actually built the fence. It was an existing structure. But she took me to court, and they ruled in her favor. I had to pay to remove the fence and rebuild it on my property line." His fingers clenched into angry fists for a tense moment before they released.

"Wow, that's a lot," Lou said.

"Fences aren't cheap, especially with the price of wood these days." Noah would know better than most with all the handyman jobs he did for people around town.

Chase scoffed. "Tell me about it. But that's not even the worst part."

Lou cringed. "It's not?"

"Nope. I wish it was," Chase said. "I had the city come out and mark the property lines for the new fence. But apparently, instead of building on *my* side of the *line*, they built on *her* side." The way he was emphasizing words made Lou worried about where this was going.

"And it still wasn't right?" Noah asked.

Chase held up three fingers. "Three inches on her property. Three. Inches." His face grew red as he talked about it.

"They couldn't possibly blame you for that. The builders were just following the property line laid out by the city." Lou grew irritated for him as she learned more about the situation.

Chase barked out another laugh, as if he had to find the humor in it, or he would just be mad. "You would think. But she took me to court *again,* and the judge said it was too likely that I built it the three inches over in retaliation for the first suit."

"So you took down the fence?" Noah guessed.

"So I took down the fence," Chase confirmed. "And then, that horrible woman had the gall to complain to me about how there was no longer any fence, so she had to take her precious little dog out on a *leash,* and didn't I know he had IBS and needed to go out multiple times during the night?" Chase made his voice high pitched as he imitated Nina's complaint.

Chase's mention of the leash, and the emphasis he'd used

when talking about it, piqued Lou's interest. Even though Detective Anderson and the medical examiner had concluded the killer was likely around Lou's size in order to resort to using the leash as a choking implement, that didn't mean it was out of the question that a larger person could've used the leash instead of their hands. Lou looked Chase up and down. The use of the leash as a murder weapon might've been more symbolic than due to necessity.

Lou stared ahead at the open space between the two houses as she took in Chase's story. As someone who'd had a not-so-pleasant interaction with Nina, Lou was almost glad to hear that she hadn't been the only one who the woman had come after. There was nothing worse than arguing with a person whom everyone else liked.

But as nice as it was to know she wasn't alone, Lou realized the other implications of Chase's story. Namely, that the mystery texter had definitely been right to send her in this direction. If Detective Anderson thought Lou had a motive, it was nothing compared to Chase's. He had endured months of frustration, spent tens of thousands of dollars, and was losing a home he loved.

"Wow, Chase. I'm so sorry. That sounds frustrating." Noah placed a supportive hand on Chase's shoulder.

The man gave his neighbor a half-hearted smile. "What can you do? My daughter has an extra room. I'm going to move in with her until I can get my feet back under me. It didn't help that I had to take so many days off work to deal with the legal issues and now with trying to sell the place." At that, he turned and looked at Lou and then at Noah. "Did I hear you say you might be interested in buying it?"

Noah opened his mouth, but Lou jumped in before he could say anything.

"No. Sorry. We just wanted to make sure you were okay," Lou blurted, not wanting Chase to get his hopes up about possibly finding a buyer. The man had been through enough.

Though, if he's a killer, I'm not sure I should care so much about his feelings, Lou thought.

She immediately scolded herself. There was about as much evidence pointing to Chase as there was pointing to her. She shouldn't jump to conclusions, lest she became like everything she despised about Detective Anderson.

Hearing that they weren't interested in buying, Chase glanced back at his house like he had things to be doing instead of rehashing his frustrating past with his neighbor. Sure their candid time with him was ending, Lou racked her brain for any last-minute questions she could ask Chase to help determine if he'd had the opportunity to kill Nina.

But if Nina had been killed in the wee hours of the morning, like Detective Anderson had implied, anyone could've done it. "I was at home, asleep" wasn't something anyone could really verify, especially for people who lived alone like Chase or Lou.

She would have to find some other way to prove it was—or wasn't—Chase.

"We won't keep you any longer," Lou said, holding up her hand in a quick wave. "Thank you for chatting with us, and best of luck with your house sale."

He returned the gesture. "Thank you. Though having a woman murdered next door isn't exactly going to help things along. It looks like Nina got me one last time."

Lou felt bad for the man, but she suddenly thought of one more thing she wanted to ask him before they left. "Your leaves," she said. "They've been raked and taken away."

Chase studied Lou, obviously unsure where she was going

with that thought. "Wanted the yard to be neat in case buyers stopped by."

"Did you see the bags get picked up by the yard waste people?" Noah asked.

Chase shook his head. "I didn't see it, but they were gone Monday morning when I woke up, so I assumed."

Lou and Noah shared a pointed look, one Chase read all too clearly.

His lips parted. "You don't think it was my leaves that they used to cover her?" He shivered.

"It seems likely since her yard wasn't raked," Lou explained. "They would've been easy enough for someone to grab and toss over her."

Chase shivered again, and Lou wondered if it was for their benefit or if he'd suddenly changed his mind about how he felt about Nina's death.

Noah and Lou parted ways with Chase at the sidewalk as he returned to his porch, and they walked toward Noah's place.

"That was..." Noah started.

"Informative, but also somehow not exactly what we need-ed," Lou supplied when it didn't seem like Noah could grasp which words to describe the interaction they'd just had with Nina's angry neighbor.

"Exactly." Noah puffed out his cheeks. "On one hand, he definitely had cause to hate Nina."

"On the other, Nina's death isn't good for his chances of selling that house quickly," Lou added.

Noah tapped his nose. "Exactly."

Lou was about to bring up the difficulties created by the time of death when her phone buzzed with an incoming text. It was from Willow.

What are you up to tonight? Easton and I ordered pizza, but they got the order wrong and brought an extra one.

"Sorry, it's Willow," Lou told Noah to excuse herself for being on her phone for a moment.

Noah nodded. "No problem."

Lou tapped the side of her phone as she considered the offer. She was hungry, and pizza was always welcome in her world. Normally, she wouldn't have hesitated for a split second if Willow invited her over. But the addition of Easton made her feel like it might be a date.

Are you sure the two of you don't want to be alone?

Willow responded immediately.

We spent the last hour doing yard work. We're tired and a little sore. You're not interrupting anything romantic.

Lou glanced over at Noah as they approached his house. He'd given her space while she'd been texting, and she did a double take as she got an idea.

Mind if I bring Noah? I haven't asked him yet, but he was helping me with something, and I think he might be free.

Willow sent back,

The more the merrier!

Lou tucked her phone away and looked over at Noah. "Do

you have dinner plans?"

Noah perked up. "There's a leftover container of soup in the fridge that I could eat. Why?"

"Willow and Easton got an extra pizza delivered by accident and want help eating it all. Want to join us?" Lou gestured to her phone as evidence that it was what Willow had been texting her about.

"I'm good at helping finish food." He smiled, his dimple showing up again. "I'd love to. Want me to drive?"

"I can drive," Lou said. "I'm enjoying my newfound freedom too much."

Noah climbed in when she unlocked the car. "That's right. I forgot that you never had a car in New York City. How's it treating you?" He ran a hand over the dashboard.

"It's lovely, but I need to up my running distance to make up for not walking, now that I'm driving this everywhere I need to go." Until that month, Lou had walked most places in Button, unless Willow drove her.

"I hear you." Noah patted his stomach, which made a hollow sound like it was still taut and muscled despite his complaints. "I do so much building during the spring and summer months that I really should up my time in the gym when it's colder to compensate, but the last thing I want to do is work out when it's rainy like this."

They arrived at Willow's. For a moment, Lou wondered which house to pull up to. Willow and Easton shared a driveway. It branched off to their separate homes at the last fifty feet. But she didn't see any lights on in Easton's house, and Willow's emitted a soft yellow glow in the setting sun.

The smell of pizza met them along with Willow's infectious laugh as they walked inside.

"Yay!" Willow waved them over. "Come, grab a slice."

Easton stood and gave Lou a hug and Noah a handshake.

After serving themselves, the four friends sat around Willow's dining table.

"Easton, how's your case going?" Noah asked. "I can't believe something like this happened to Judge Potts. I mean, he had a reputation for being strict, but to have someone shoot him? That's unimaginable."

Easton leaned back in his chair. "As much as I'm tempted to believe it has to do with him being a judge—which we're definitely checking into—it seems more likely that Becky did it."

"His wife?" Willow let her piece of pizza drop away from her mouth before she took another bite.

"Her story doesn't check out. She said she stayed the night with a friend in Seattle, but that friend is conveniently out of town now, on some yacht in the French Riviera, and I can't get ahold of her to corroborate that story."

"Well, it's hard to prove where you were at three in the morning," Lou grumbled.

Willow patted her friend on the back. She turned to Easton. "Don't mind her. She's just a little sour about Roy and how much he's been going after her in Nina's murder case."

"I'm sorry." Easton pinched the bridge of his nose for a moment. "I will say that Roy rubs people the wrong way because he's just not all that likable, but he is a good detective. He'll find out the truth."

"I hope so," Lou said.

"I heard he was following up with the phone company about that number," Easton continued. "He's using the information you're giving him. He's just bad at showing gratitude."

Or he's hoping the number is somehow connected to me so he can arrest me, Lou thought to herself.

At that moment, her phone buzzed with a text message.

Lou's eyes went wide since the person who texted her most was sitting next to her at the dinner table. Willow's attention cut over to the phone in question, equally confused.

It could be one of her nieces. They communicated with her primarily via text or video calls. It could also be her parents, who'd spent the last year retiring, selling their house, and buying an RV that they were driving across the country. Now that they had more time on their hands, they were using a lot of that to call and check in on their only daughter. But there was a pit in Lou's stomach as she considered the possibility that it could be her mystery texter.

That fear sent spikes of heat up her neck as she glanced at the screen and saw the now-familiar number without a name attached to it.

Keep going.

Her heart raced. So the texter had seen her talk to Chase today. Keep going? Did that mean that she was on the right track or that she had the wrong neighbor?

"Lou, you look like you just got a message from a ghost." Easton wiped his mouth with a napkin and laughed.

Willow pressed her lips together and pretended to be really interested in her pizza.

Easton's laughter cut short. "Wait. Is it from—"

"It is." Lou had considered lying but knew she needed to be open and honest with her friends.

"If they won't leave you alone, you can block their number." Easton held out his hand. "I can show you how to do it."

"Wait. Who won't leave you alone?" Noah asked, his dark eyebrows pulling tight.

Lou gripped her phone tighter. "It's not—" She stopped, unsure of what to say. "I don't want to block them."

Easton's eyes widened. "You mean you're still in contact with the person?"

"What person?" Noah started to sound frustrated. "Who are we talking about?"

Lou glanced from Easton's disappointed expression to Noah's concerned one. Deciding Noah's was the safer option, she held his gaze as she said, "Someone's messaging me clues about Nina's death. They're the one who told me to question Chase Humphrey. And they just sent me a text saying I should keep going."

CHAPTER 9

Noah appeared to go through about a dozen different emotions in the following moments. But the most prominent emotion, and the one he settled on, seemed to be confusion.

"Why would someone be talking to you and not the police?" Noah asked.

"Exactly," Easton said, holding out a hand toward Noah in a *listen to this guy* gesture.

Lou peeked over at Willow, hoping for support, but from the tight set of her shoulders, Lou could see that her friend was more likely to be concerned for her safety than side with her on this.

"The person said they can't go to the police because they don't have all the information. They need my help to patch the holes with clues, so there's clear evidence pointing to the culprit." Lou tried to sound surer than she was about her mystery texter's motives.

"You're being generous. Show him the texts." Easton snapped his fingers.

Lou pulled up the conversation and pushed the phone toward Noah. His eyes flicked over the screen, and then he looked over at Easton.

"It could be the killer, luring her into a trap because they think she knows too much," Easton said.

Noah squinted one eye. "He's right, Lou. This doesn't sound like a mentally stable person. The fact that they won't answer your questions about who they are or why they can't go to the police is concerning. And they obviously watched us talk to Chase Humphrey today."

"Which was a good lead." Lou opened her hand, palm up. "He definitely had a motive to kill her."

Easton tsked as he read the latest text. "I can't believe you're taking directions from this person. At least you had Noah with you today. But that doesn't mean he can be with you at all times. What if they come after you in the bookshop or follow you on one of your runs?"

Lou let her shoulders slump forward. "I got desperate when Detective Anderson came to my house with that warrant."

"Will you just promise us you won't go investigating alone?" Willow said, reaching out to grab on to Lou's arm. She gave it a gentle squeeze.

"Willow, you can't seriously be supporting this?" Easton's question was full of disappointment.

Willow shrugged. "I've known Lou most of my life. I know she's an independent thinker who's going to do what she thinks is right. That's part of why I love her." She smiled at her friend. "And I know that she won't listen just because you tell her not to do something. Not because she's reckless, but because Lou knows more than most people that danger finds you even when you do everything right."

Lou met her friend's gaze. They shared a sad look, mourning

Benjamin, Lou's late husband. Ben had been super health-conscious. He ran almost every day. And yet he'd still had a heart attack before the age of forty. What good was running from danger when it could find you anyway?

Lou placed a hand on Willow's and squeezed.

Easton's frustration ticked a muscle in his jaw one last time before he exhaled it away. "Okay. Fine. You know my worries. You can do what you want." He took another bite of his pizza, chewed, and swallowed before adding, "Willow's right. Take someone with you anytime you're investigating or following one of their texts, and *never* meet if they ask you to meet."

"They really don't seem like the kind to ask that." Lou wrinkled her nose. "They seem pretty antisocial."

Easton pointed his slice of pizza toward her. "Mark my words. In the next couple of days, they'll ask you to meet. That will be your clue that they're the murderer."

Lou was sure they wouldn't ask.

"So what did they mean by keep going?" Noah asked, sliding Lou's phone back toward her. "Is Chase the right person, and we need to keep talking to him, or are we supposed to talk to more neighbors? Does the person think it's the neighbor that killed Nina, or do the neighbors have the clues that'll point us to the murderer?"

"All valid questions," Willow said.

Lou agreed. "I wondered the same thing when it first came through. Let's see what they'll tell us." She typed out a response.

She showed the text to everyone at the table. Willow and Noah gave her nods of encouragement. Easton huffed. She sent the message.

Lou studied the screen for the next few seconds, waiting for an answer. The others watched Lou.

But nothing came through. Lou set the phone on the table and turned her attention back to her pizza. She took another bite, chewing in the ensuing silence.

"So..." Willow said, obviously trying to fill the silence. "I saw a sign that the pumpkin patch out on Linen Drive is open. Anyone want to have a fall fun day?" She turned to Lou. "They have a cool corn maze on the property too."

Lou squeezed her elbows into her sides with excitement. "You know I'm always in for a fall fun day."

If she were being honest, she was missing New York City in the fall a little more than she thought she would. Her condo had been close to Central Park, and she'd loved running through, watching the foliage change as the temperature dropped.

Easton coughed. "I mean, I like a corn maze as much as the next guy. I'd be in." He glanced up at Willow, a slight smile tugging at the corners of his lips for the first time since their conversation had taken a turn for the frustrating.

Noah raised his hand. "If you don't mind someone who will most definitely get lost in the maze, I'm down for a fall fun day."

Willow chuckled. "Just stick with Lou. She remembers all the details. She'll get you out. That's what I always do."

"Now you have me," Easton said, sticking out his chest. "Don't worry. I'm very good at mazes."

Lou's heart just about melted for her friend and the cute way Easton had just offered to get her through the maze.

"Does Marigold want to come with?" Lou asked Noah.

"She would love that," he said. "I have her Thursday through Sunday this week." Noah and his ex-wife shared custody in what, to Lou and the other Button locals, seemed like the most cordial custody agreement ever.

They made plans to go the next night, Thursday, and were just doing the dishes when Lou's phone buzzed.

All four of them stopped short and trained their eyes on the table. Lou walked over, picking up the phone. She gulped as she turned on the screen and read the response to herself.

Different neighbor. Killer.

A chill wound down her spine despite the coziness of her best friend's house.

"Well, what did they say?" Willow asked, her tone sharp with impatience.

Lou relayed the text to them. They contemplated the meaning of the cryptic words. Each person seemed disturbed in their own way.

Easton's phone rang, startling everyone. He moved into the other room to take the call. Lou, Noah, and Willow worked on putting away the dishes and leftover pizza while he talked.

He came back into the room a moment later, his jacket in hand.

"Gotta go." He pulled on the jacket while walking over to Willow and planting a kiss on her cheek, causing her to blush. Then, looking at Lou, he said, "Do not meet that person. No matter what."

With that, he was gone.

"What are you going to say in response?" Willow asked Lou, refocusing on the eerie message they'd just received.

"Can you ask them which neighbor?" Noah asked.

Lou wrinkled her nose. "I've asked them pointed questions before, but they wouldn't answer."

"It might be worth asking this one." Noah shrugged.

She typed her response.

Which neighbor?

They waited. Nothing happened.

Noah chewed on his lip and then sat down at the table once more. He took one of Willow's notepads from her coffee table and flipped it to a blank page. Drawing parallel lines, he put squares on either side, like a neighborhood. On the square in the corner he wrote an N. To the left of that one he put a C.

"Nina. Chase." Lou pointed to each one as she caught Willow up on the map.

"This is Lester Frazier here." He put an L in the house behind Nina's. "Across the street, we have Melissa, Terrance, and their two kids. Melissa's younger brother, Omer, just moved in with them too." He marked those with their initials as well.

"What do you know about these people?" Willow asked.

Noah puffed out his cheeks. "Not whether any of them is capable of murder, unfortunately."

"What's this little box you drew here?" Willow asked, pointing to the map.

"Oh, that's Omer's tiny house. He parks it in the RV slip next to his sister's driveway." Noah placed an O in the smaller rectangle.

Lou studied the ceiling as she tried to remember seeing something like that. "I must've been distracted. I don't think I even looked across the street."

"Tiny house? Like on HGTV?" Willow asked from the kitchen.

Noah tipped his head from side to side. "Sort of. It's on a large trailer bed. He's living inside while he's working on building the interior. He loves chatting about what he's doing and giving tours." Noah scratched at his chin. "Showed Marigold all the cool little space savers he's designed over the years. She's convinced she's going to live in a tiny house when she grows up, now. It's all she talked about for the next week."

"Any of these people match my physical description, since Detective Anderson seems to think I'm the prime suspect since I'm smaller and would've used a leash to strangle Nina instead of with my hands?" Lou asked.

Noah coughed in discomfort for a second, then said, "Yeah, pretty much everyone but Chase. Melissa's husband, Terrance, is pretty tall. But she and Omer are closer to your height. So is Lester Frazier."

"So, who should we look into first?" Willow asked. "Since *Clues McGee* isn't coming through with any specifics." She gestured to Lou's still silent phone.

Noah blinked. "Your guess would be as good as mine. They all seem like normal folks."

"Then we pick them off the list one by one," Lou said, folding the paper and sticking it in her purse.

"Should we keep Chase on our radar?" Noah asked. "Since your source seems to think it's not him?"

Lou pursed her lips as she thought. "He stays on the list. He hated Nina and lives right next door to her."

"Oooh," Willow dragged out the word like the high school students in her previous job might have if someone was asked to go to the principal's office. "Going against your mystery texter?"

Lou didn't let it bother her, though. "Again, this mystery texter is only helping. I don't know who they are or if they're right, but it's worth seeing what they have to say."

She just hoped it was worth it.

CHAPTER 10

About halfway through the day on Thursday, Lou's phone buzzed with a text message. She stiffened. Would it be another communication from the mystery texter?

The bookshop had been absolutely jumping all morning, which meant so had Lou—specifically, after Holden Clawfield to thwart his escape attempts. Probably because of this continued activity, the little guy was actually fast asleep on the fleece cat bed Noah and Marigold had made for him.

Between Holden being momentarily still and Silas her only customer, Lou felt like she could take the moment to check her phone.

Anticipation tightened every muscle in her body as she picked up her phone and flipped it over. An exhale of expectation whooshed out of Lou as she saw the text was from Willow.

> Do you want Easton to swing by and pick you up on our way out to the pumpkin patch today?

She considered her friend's offer. While kind, Lou knew

Easton and Willow hadn't had as much time alone as they'd hoped lately. She had her own car now. It would be fun to venture out farther into the surrounding area.

> Thanks, but I think I might drive myself. I'll meet you there!

Just as she was putting down her phone, the shop door opened. Lou stiffened, watching Holden Clawfield to make sure he didn't bolt. While he remained fast asleep, Lou didn't relax. The person who walked inside the bookshop was Detective Roy Anderson.

He scanned the space as if he might be in possession of another search warrant.

"Detective, how can I help you today?" Lou asked in the kindest tone she could muster.

Silas glanced up at Lou's change in demeanor.

"Oh, just checking on a few things." He perused her new-release display as if he was there to buy a book.

"We can see right through you," Silas grumbled, folding his newspaper into his lap. "Don't you think you're going to get anything on our Lou. She's as clean as they come." He set his chin and winked toward Lou.

Her heart warmed at his support.

"Sure, she was spitting mad that day when Nina came in here, and she loves that cat more than anything else in this world, but you can't prove a thing." Silas jabbed a stubby finger toward Detective Anderson.

Lou inwardly groaned, wishing that Silas would support her a little less.

"Interesting." Detective Anderson stepped forward. "When you say *spitting mad*, how would you characterize that?" He pulled out a notebook and a pen, ready to write.

Silas glanced worriedly at Lou, realizing his mistake. "Uh, well, the woman's spent the last two decades living in New York City. She's hard as nails."

Lou pressed her palms onto the register counter and tried to steady her breathing.

"In a good way," Silas added quickly. "She doesn't take guff from anyone. Doesn't let 'em walk all over her." Silas nodded resolutely, as if he was sure that would fix it.

Detective Anderson studied Lou for a moment before turning his attention back toward Silas. "Since you're so sure she's innocent, you wouldn't mind telling me exactly what you saw and heard the day of the interaction between Lou and Nina, would you?"

Silas sent Lou a questioning look. She waved a hand toward him, telling him to go ahead. The detective already knew about the fight. Hearing the details from Silas wouldn't put her in any deeper trouble, she hoped.

But by the time Detective Anderson left, Lou was exhausted. So when she got a text from Noah an hour later, her determination to drive herself crumbled.

You driving with Willow and Easton, or do you want to catch a ride with me and Marigold? Apparently, there's some new series she has to discuss with you. Something to do with cat dragons?

Lou felt a lightness come over her as she remembered how shy Marigold had been the first time she'd met her. Now she could barely get the girl to *stop* talking.

Sure. I'd love a ride. I'll be ready after I close.

Noah sent back a thumbs-up, and Lou turned her attention to a customer who'd been sitting on the love seat, looking through a stack of books for the last few minutes.

The woman set the entire stack of books on the counter and pushed them toward Lou.

"I was deciding between these two." The woman gestured to the books on the top of the pile. "But I couldn't make my mind up, so I've decided to get five instead." An excited grin spread over her face.

Lou cackled. "Oh, I know that decision-making strategy well." She rang up the woman's purchases and said goodbye, eyeing Holden like a hawk in case he woke and bolted for the open door.

But the little flame-point Siamese stayed put and Lou relaxed. Alone in her shop, she glanced over at the children's section of the bookshop and scanned the new releases, trying to think of the series Marigold might be referring to. With the narrow criteria that it was a new series and it involved cat dragons, it wasn't hard for Lou to locate the books.

The sleepy afternoon that followed afforded her time to check out the first book in the series. She'd read almost halfway through the thing before she locked the door and turned the sign in the window. The cats yawned and stretched, following her upstairs as she exchanged the Birkenstocks she wore around the bookstore for her warmest pair of boots.

It was chilly out there, and she knew she'd need the extra layers if they were going to be wandering around outside in the corn maze and in search of pumpkins. Noah texted.

Just leaving the clinic. On my way to you.

Heading downstairs now.

Once she was sure the cats were happy and fed upstairs, she grabbed a wool jacket and went to stand outside the bookshop to wait for Noah. His truck pulled to a stop in front of her a minute later, and she climbed in the passenger side.

"I thought I'd have a little more time to run home first, but my last appointment went over. Do you mind if I swing by the house? I need to grab Marigold's boots and change into mine." Noah winced apologetically.

"I don't mind at all," Lou said. "You two are going to want those boots in this weather." She rubbed her hands up and down her arms.

Noah had the heater blasting in the truck, but it had obviously been sitting in the cold parking lot of the clinic while he saw patients all day, and it wasn't quite warm.

"Thanks," he said, pulling out onto Thread Lane. After navigating through the roundabout in the center of downtown, he took a right up Pattern Drive toward his neighborhood.

Lou couldn't help but let her gaze linger on Nina Upton's house as they drove by.

"Huh. That's weird," Noah said.

Peeling her attention from Nina's place, Lou expected Noah to be looking in the same direction as she was. But he slowed the truck as he stared out the driver's side window.

The house across the street from Nina's was a well-kept red cottage with a beautiful front garden. That wasn't the most interesting thing about the place, though. Parked in the RV slip next to the driveway of the house was a tiny version of the same house. It was also painted red, with similar cream-colored trim. Unlike the larger version, this one had a tow hitch attached to the front, and it sat on a trailer bed.

"Oh, is that the tiny house you mentioned yesterday?" Lou

asked, leaning forward to get a better look as they slowly inched by.

Noah cocked his head. "Yeah. That's it. But the weird thing is that it's got a for-sale sign on the front."

Lou didn't need to search long to notice the large sign advertising All Offers Considered. "He's selling it? I thought you said he adored that thing?" The same confusion that was plaguing Noah transferred to Lou.

"He does—did, I guess." Noah shook his head and kept driving. "That's super weird."

For a split second, Lou wondered if he might be selling because he didn't want to live next to the scene of a murder. But she caught herself, almost laughing at her silliness. If he didn't want to live there, his house had wheels. He could move it somewhere else.

"Maybe he's a tiny-house flipper," she suggested. "You said he's been working on the inside while he's living there. Maybe he's finally done, is going to sell it, and start on a new one."

Noah lifted his fingers off the steering wheel for a second in a small-scale shrug. "Maybe."

He parked in his driveway and told her he wouldn't be more than a few minutes inside, giving her the choice to wait in the truck or come into the house.

"I'll wait here," she said.

She stared out the window, looking at the neighborhood, thinking of the hand-drawn map Noah had made, contemplating her mystery texter's certainty that the killer was one of Nina's neighbors.

Noah jogged out minutes later, wearing warmer boots and carrying a small pair for his daughter. "Okay," he said as he slid back into the driver's seat. "Marigold's club is just finishing up." He drove toward the elementary school.

Marigold waited among a group of students and two teachers as they pulled up to Button Elementary. She pointed and jumped up and down as she recognized her dad's truck.

Opening the passenger door, Lou climbed out so she could let Marigold into the back seat.

"You're driving with us?" Marigold's excitement was electric, so much so that Lou half expected to get a static shock when the little girl touched her hand, climbing into the truck.

"Of course," Lou said with a smile. "I hear we have a lot to talk about."

Marigold's eyes went wide. She nodded seriously as she buckled herself in, and Noah pulled away from the curb. "I found a new series I think you're going to love."

Lou waited, knowing that, even if she had guessed the series correctly, she didn't want to take away the joy of recommending a great book from Marigold. Lou listened seriously as Marigold told her the name of the series. A grin peeled over Lou's face as she turned to look at the little girl.

"I just started it today. You're right! I'm loving it," Lou gushed.

Marigold squealed with delight. "What's your favorite part?"

Noah chuckled. "Petal, what have we said about making that high-pitched noise in the car?" he asked gently.

Marigold pressed her lips together. "Sorry, Dad. But it's *so* good."

"Yeah," Lou teased, "you can't predict reactions when we're talking cat dragons. And my favorite part is definitely how they change color to fit their mood."

She and Marigold chatted animatedly, though at a more acceptable pitch for driving, the rest of the way.

When Lou, Noah, and Marigold finally pulled up to the

pumpkin patch, Willow and Easton were waiting for them by the small stand where customers could buy tickets to the corn maze or weigh and pay for their pumpkins.

Willow walked forward, balancing three cups of steaming liquid. "I got you ciders." She handed one cup to Lou and another to Marigold.

The spicy scent of cinnamon and nutmeg greeted Lou first, followed up by the sweetness of the apple juice. Lou wrapped her fingers around the warm paper cup and held it under her nose so she could breathe in the lovely smell.

"Thank you," Lou and Marigold said at the same time.

Easton held a cup out toward Noah, and they were officially all equipped with ciders.

"We already paid for everyone to do the corn maze," Willow said. "Should we do that first, and then we can pick out pumpkins?"

Everyone agreed with Willow's plan. After making sure Marigold didn't need to use the restroom, they followed the whimsical hand-painted signs toward a field of seven-foot-tall stalks of corn. They stood next to a large sign, made from a wooden pallet with rules painted on each slat, that outlined expectations for the corn maze, reading as they drank their cider.

No running.

Stay on paths.

No swearing (remember, the corn has ears).

Do not pick the corn.

Both directions lead to an exit.

"Sounds simple enough." Lou placed her hands on her hips.

"Maybe too simple..." A mischievous grin overtook Willow's normally pleasant expression.

"What does that mean?" Noah asked, a hint of worry in his tone.

"Race!" Marigold raised both arms as if her team was already the winner. "Whoever came in a car together is on a team," she said as quickly as she could, like someone else might beat her to a different suggestion. She reached out and grabbed Lou and Noah by the hand.

Willow cocked an eyebrow. "Oh, Marigold. You've made a huge mistake." She tapped Easton on the chest. "This here is a detective. He notices everything. He has instincts like a jungle cat. And that's not even the best part."

Marigold leaned forward, waiting in awe to learn what that might be. Lou swore she saw Easton lean forward, too, wanting to know possibly even more than the child.

"I can talk to plants. And corn is a plant. The stalks are going to tell me where to go." Willow pushed her shoulders back.

Marigold's eyes widened. Hearing the last part wasn't about him, Easton's shoulders sank forward a few inches.

"Can plants really talk?" Marigold asked her father.

Noah sent an exasperated scowl toward Willow.

"Well, basically." Willow lifted her chin. "They have their own special language. And I'm fluent in it."

"That's why you're opening up your Willow nursery." Marigold nodded as if this made all the sense in the world.

"Right." Willow tossed her empty cup into the nearby trash can. "Last group out buys the pumpkins," Willow said, grabbing Easton's hand and rushing into the maze.

Lou, Noah, and Marigold followed, taking a right where Willow and Easton had taken a left. Marigold's laughter each time they stopped at a crossroads and decided which way to go made it all worth it, win or lose.

But about halfway through, Marigold tugged on Noah's arm. "Daddy, I need to use the bathroom." She crossed her legs.

Frustration flickered over Noah's features for the briefest of moments. He had asked her before they started the maze. But any hardness in his body language quickly softened. "Okay, Petal." He peered forward, craning his neck a bit as if it would help him see over the tall cornstalks. "I think our best bet is to go back the way we came, though, since we know there's a bathroom there, and I'm not sure if there's one at the end of the maze."

Marigold danced around, agreeing with the need for the closest bathroom.

"Do you think you can finish on your own? Get us that win?" Noah asked Lou.

She saluted him and then Marigold. "I will do my best. Good luck."

They saluted her back, and then they were off.

The sounds of chatter and laughter felt so close as other groups made their way through the expansive maze, but at the same time, they felt so far away.

Corn stalks rustled behind her. Lou shivered. She could've sworn she heard someone whisper the name Nina. "Nina. Nina. Where are you, Nina?"

An icy-cold sensation settled on the back of her neck, tingling out to her shoulders, as if someone were standing much too close.

Lou spun around, heart hammering. She was alone.

Chastising herself for being paranoid, she continued in the direction her team had been heading before bathroom needs had split them up.

Another rustling in the corn stalks behind her turned her

thoughts back to Easton's warning yesterday about how the mystery texter could very well be the murderer, and they could try to get rid of Lou for sticking her nose into the case. And there she was, alone in a corn maze. What if they were following her?

Just then, Lou tripped on something, falling forward onto her hands and knees. She scrambled away, fear spiking through her, constricting the air in her lungs, as she noticed an arm reaching through the cornstalks.

"She's right there. Get her," a woman hissed from the other side.

A masculine arm grasped at the air, almost latching on to Lou's leg. Lou crab-crawled backward, jumped again as her hand touched something that felt like a face. Gasping and glancing down, she realized it *was* a face. A doll's face had been cut out and sewn onto a purse. Legs and arms jutted unnaturally out the sides and bottom. Was this some kind of threat? A warning? Lou wasn't about to stick around to find out. She got to her feet and ignored the first rule of the corn maze.

She ran.

After a few turns, she heard voices again and saw a similar wooden archway to the one that had marked the entrance. It had Exit painted on the top.

Gasping for breath, Lou ran toward the exit. Willow and Easton stood outside, wearing smug grins. Lou grabbed for Willow, holding on to her friend's arms as her heart slowed.

"Goodness, Lou. You look like you were running from a monster in there. Don't tell me." Willow laughed preemptively. "You were being stalked. Get it? Stalked." She pointed to the stalks of corn and slapped at her knee.

But Easton's detective skills seemed to kick in a lot earlier than Willow's plant communication skills. He took a step closer to Lou, eyebrows pulling together in concern.

Lou finally caught her breath. "I think that's exactly what happened. And I think whoever it was might've killed Nina."

CHAPTER 11

After hearing about Lou's experience in the corn maze, Easton insisted he go back through and search for the people. Willow and Lou would not let him go by himself, so they went as a group of three.

"I'm sure it was a man and a woman," Lou whispered. "She was saying, 'Get her. She's right there,' and then a man's hand reached through the corn and grabbed at me. I think he was whispering Nina's name before I tripped."

"Trying to freak you out so you made a mistake?" Willow made a show of shivering. "That's creepy."

But they didn't see anyone with a similar purse made of doll parts by the time they exited the maze through the front once again.

Noah and Marigold waited for them near the pumpkin patch, a wheelbarrow ready to go. They waved to the group as they emerged from the maze.

"Who won?" Marigold asked, jumping up and down in suspense.

Willow elbowed Lou. "Your team, of course," Willow lied.

Lou shot her friend a grateful glance as Marigold celebrated. Willow obviously felt bad about what Lou had gone through in the maze. They walked forward together, entering the pumpkin patch.

There were a handful of families and a few couples wandering through, looking for their perfect gourd to carve for Halloween in just under two weeks.

"Look at this one!" Marigold skipped forward, crouching next to a pumpkin almost as big as she was.

"Is that your pick?" Willow asked nervously. Her eyes widened like she was regretting her decision to pay for the pumpkins.

But Marigold stood. "No, I want something I can carry." She cradled her arms in front of her body, showing the space where the pumpkin should fit.

"Okay, well let's go find it." Willow stepped forward, stopping and pointing. "Oh, wait. I think I see it. Is that it there?"

"No." Marigold shook her head. "But that's a perfect pumpkin for Dad."

Noah appraised the pumpkin. "Great pick, Petal."

It was in this fashion that Marigold chose everyone's pumpkins. Which was fine with Lou since she couldn't seem to stop checking over her shoulder at any sign of movement. Easton's head also seemed to be on a swivel, and his eyes narrowed each time a group walked by them, especially a woman and a man together.

When a hand landed on Lou's shoulder, she almost screamed. But the gentle weight of it stopped her. When she turned to see who it belonged to, she found Noah standing close, concern etching lines of worry into his forehead. He kept his hand on her shoulder.

"Is everything okay?" he asked as their group moved out of earshot. "You seem worried."

Lou inhaled, letting her nostrils flare. She leaned in close. "Let's just say our team did not win the maze race."

Noah's dark eyes searched her face for more clues.

"I don't want to say anything that might scare Marigold, but I think someone followed me after you two left the corn maze. It could've been my mystery texter, or it could've been the killer, or they might be the same person. I think it was a couple, though. A man and a woman." She shivered.

Noah's warm hand dropped from her shoulder. "I'm so sorry. We should never have left you alone in that maze."

"It's broad daylight," she scoffed, gesturing to the grayish sky—which was already darkening from the early setting sun, so it was generous of her to refer to it as daylight. "How could any of us predict that a corn maze could be dangerous? And anyway, they didn't hurt me. I'm okay." She focused all her energy into producing the most convincing smile she could.

It wasn't anyone's fault but her own. She'd gone against Easton's advice and had continued to contact the mystery texter. She'd been investigating Nina's death.

"I will say that I think my investment in this case has run out." She rubbed at her arms as a gust of chilly wind charged through the pumpkin patch. "The possibility of being falsely accused of murder seems much better than the idea of being the next victim."

Noah nodded somberly. "Agreed. You need to stay as far away from this case as you can."

Easton glanced behind him, noticing they were gone. Noah lifted his chin in a nonverbal *we're coming* gesture. They caught up with the group, but Lou didn't miss that Noah stayed right by her side during the rest of their time at the pumpkin patch.

ONCE THEY HAD ALL the pumpkins picked, paid for, and loaded into the vehicles, the group said its goodbyes. Marigold chattered on about the different options she was considering for her pumpkin design as Noah drove home.

Lou slid out of the truck, clutching her pumpkin, and gave the two Romeros a small wave. "Thanks for a fun evening," she said, noticing how a low fog crept through the streets of downtown Button in the deepening dark.

Noah held her gaze. And even though he only said, "See you soon," she could feel the subtext of *let me know if you need anything* as clearly as if he'd said it aloud.

She shut the door and stepped back as they pulled away. Turning toward the bookshop, warmth overcame Lou. Golden light spilled out of the front windows, highlighting the books inside. The cats were all upstairs in her apartment, so none were visible from where she stood, but she knew they would provide the perfect amount of cozy company on this chilly evening.

But before she could even walk forward to unlock the front door, a car pulled into the parking spot Noah had just vacated.

"Nice gourd," Willow called through her open window.

Lou turned to see her best friend getting out of her car.

"You didn't think I was going to let you stay here alone after a creepy day like that, did you?" Willow asked as she strode past her and pulled out her own key to the bookshop.

Lou closed her eyes for a second and exhaled in relief. She hadn't realized how much she needed company tonight until Willow showed up. She followed her best friend into the shop. They locked the front door, then headed up to Lou's apartment, greeted by Holden Clawfield. Well, "greeting" was what Lou was calling it when he waited by the door and attempted to bolt through the opening.

"Do you have anything for dinner, or should we order in?" Willow asked, dropping her bag on the couch and walking straight for the fridge.

"What about OC and Steve? Don't they need dinner?" Lou asked.

Willow opened the fridge. "I cleaned the stalls earlier, and Easton said he'd feed them for me."

Lou couldn't argue with that. She forgot that while Willow was locked in to doing her barn chores early in the morning or in the evenings when she worked at the high school, she had time during the day right now while she set up her nursery.

"I have pasta. Want to do that?" Lou suggested, resigned to the comforting fact that there was no getting rid of Willow tonight.

"Perfect." Willow pulled out the ingredients.

They chatted as they worked on dinner together. At first, they talked about Marigold's adorable antics at the farm earlier, but they'd skirted the topic long enough, and Willow finally broke.

"How are you feeling about what happened?" she asked.

Lou paused in her dinner prep, placing her hands on the counter as concern surrounding her cornstalk encounter hit again. She wasn't sure how to answer Willow's question.

"Like, does it make you want to work harder at the mystery or stay away?" Willow clarified, seeing her friend couldn't find the words.

"Stay away, for sure." Lou cut the air with her palm. "I was trying to help save myself from being wrongfully accused of murder, but this is way worse. I'm out of the investigation," she said definitively.

Willow studied her, as if she wasn't sure if that was the whole truth. "Okay. What can I do to help?"

Lou brought the dishes of pasta to the table. "Give me something else to focus on." Lou sat and served herself once Willow had taken some. "What's going on with the nursery? Can I help you? That would keep my mind off Nina's case."

Willow launched into a list of the things she'd accomplished: she'd signed the lease for the property on Needle Street yesterday, had greenhouses on order, and had a quote for fencing that would encompass the nursery so she could lock up her stock at night. Then she launched into the longer list of everything still needing to be done: ordering the rest of her seeds, getting grow lights so she could work on starts, and working out a watering system that used the space efficiently.

"And that's not even mentioning the enormous task of finding land on which to grow everything," Willow said with a hard swallow.

"Nothing else you've looked at works?" Lou asked, then took a bite.

Willow set down her fork in defeat. "I toured three different places yesterday, and while they'd be okay, it's going to take a lot to get the soil up to growing conditions. Or I'll need to pay a lot more to order fertilizer." Willow let her head fall forward. "Maybe I just need to give up this dream of growing everything myself. Most nurseries these days get stock delivered, and it's fine. Maybe I should just conform and do the same."

Sadness filled Lou on behalf of her friend. Willow had been dreaming of owning her own nursery since they were little. One of the most prominent parts of that dream had been Willow selling the plants she'd grown. She wanted to cut out the middleman and only sell stock she knew was healthy.

"I'll support whatever you choose to do," Lou said, "but

don't give up on that part of your dream yet. It's such an important part of your vision, and I think it's going to happen. We'll make it happen."

Willow gave Lou a half-hearted smile. Then she added, "Oh, and I realized I'm going to need an office of some sort. Noah's building me a bunch of display tables, and he said he could make a covered bar for me, to act as a checkout counter but I feel like I need something more sturdy, like a place to lock up my documents and have a computer for ordering."

Lou tipped her head to the side. "Like a little garden shed or…?"

Willow took a bite and shrugged. Once she swallowed, she said, "Yeah, or maybe even a trailer?"

Excitement wound up through Lou. "I think I know where you can find the perfect thing."

Willow cocked an eyebrow in question.

"How does a tiny house sound?"

"Like the one Noah was talking about yesterday?" Willow asked.

"Exactly that one," Lou said. "It's for sale. I saw it today. It looks like a tiny red cottage with cream trim." She wrinkled her nose at the end of the sentence.

"What's that face for? Is it expensive?" Willow leaned forward as if she'd already gotten her hopes up.

"I honestly don't know how much it is. The sign says All Offers Accepted." Lou scratched at the side of her nose. "But the guy selling it is technically one of Nina's neighbors, so going to talk to him wouldn't be staying far away from the case."

"Psh." Willow waved a hand toward Lou. "It's a small town. You can't be expected to stay away from Pattern Drive forever."

"Okay," Lou said, but there was still a hint of hesitation in her heart.

"Or I can go alone," Willow added, noticing her friend's body language.

"That's not it," Lou said. "I love my shop, but for the first time, when I thought of going through a whole day tomorrow, I felt exhausted already."

A big part of her fatigue was due to Holden Clawfield. The cat had taken to meow-screaming and clawing dramatically at Lou's sweater any time she tried to pry him away from the open door. She'd even tried locking him upstairs in her apartment, but he hated being sequestered from the other cats so much that he yowled loudly enough to be heard down in the bookshop.

"Why don't you take a day off?" Willow suggested. "A mental health day."

Lou frowned. "It's Friday tomorrow."

Willow placed her hands on her hips. "So? Your biggest days are Saturday and Sunday, right?"

Lou nodded.

"You don't even close all day on Monday and Tuesday. You haven't had a full day off in a while." Willow pointed her fork at Lou and then stabbed it into a piece of pasta.

"That's true." Lou considered it. "Maybe one day wouldn't be so bad."

She very much doubted that one day off would solve her problems, but it was worth a try.

CHAPTER 12

The next morning, Lou and Willow woke up early and went on a run. Lou knew Willow was humoring her because she normally hated running, especially when it was cold and a little rainy. But Lou enjoyed the company, even if it was slightly whiny company.

Once back at the bookshop, they got ready for a day of nursery prep. Lou was excited to have jobs to keep her mind off the case. A day off reading with the cats sounded relaxing, but it would be too easy to let her mind wander to her creepy corn maze encounter and her worries about Detective Anderson's interest in her as a suspect in Nina's murder.

With a goal to leave before the shop was supposed to open, Lou grabbed the laminated sign she'd made for the times she'd tried closing early on Mondays and Tuesdays during the spring and summer. It said: *Whiskers and Words is closed for the day. Apologies for the inconvenience. Please call the number below if there are any book-or-cat-related emergencies.* Then her cell phone was listed in the space below. She'd added that last part to gauge how many customers were really put out by her closing early on those days.

She'd only ever received two calls during that time. Lou's hand flew to her chest as she did a double-take at the sign.

"What?" Willow stepped closer. "Did you find a typo or something?"

Lou would've laughed if she didn't have a terrible, eerie feeling crawling over her skin. She shook her head and pointed to her phone number on the bottom of the page.

"Remember when we couldn't figure out how the mystery texter had gotten my phone number?" She glanced over at Willow, wild-eyed.

Willow's mouth parted in understanding. "This is your cell, not the shop phone," she said.

"I can't bring the shop phone with me when I leave since it's wired, so I put my personal cell for emergencies," Lou explained.

Willow frowned. "Did anyone ever call?"

"Noah called once, when Jules Purrn's owner decided he wanted to adopt," Lou said.

"Oh, right." Willow tapped her fingertips against her lips. "While we were working on the Spring Fling prep. I remember that."

"And one other person called." Lou tried to remember the circumstances of the other call. "It was a man who had ordered a special hardback set of a popular fantasy series. It was expensive, so it didn't surprise me when he said he'd changed his mind and wanted to cancel the order. He called because he wanted to catch me early in hopes I hadn't ordered it yet."

"That's considerate." Willow gave a quick nod of approval. "Do you remember his name?"

"Not off the top of my head. I can look up the order in my

system." Lou glanced over at her computer. But the minutes were ticking closer to opening time, and Lou didn't want to be around to confuse customers who saw the sign but also saw her inside the shop. "I can do that later. We should get going."

Willow taped the sign to the front window while Lou made sure she locked everything.

"You know, anyone walking by could've copied that number," Willow mentioned, jabbing a thumb back toward the front door and the sign with Lou's cell phone number on it.

"True." Lou chewed on her lip. "But I haven't put that up for months. How would the killer know to have my number just in case they killed Nina?"

"Unless they were planning it for a long time," Willow said ominously. "But it doesn't matter. You're staying out of things."

"Right," Lou said as they piled into Willow's car and headed for Omer's tiny house.

Willow gasped in delight as she pulled up to the house. "Oh, you're right. It's perfect."

"It'll be perfect in a nursery, like a little garden gnome lives there," Lou smiled.

"Or a tall woman is crouched inside, crunching numbers for her business." Willow cackled at the mental image.

As if she hadn't thought about having to crouch until she said that, Willow walked up to the tiny house to measure herself against the roof. Even though it was technically a "tiny house," it appeared that six-foot Willow would still be able to stand comfortably inside. Willow tried knocking on the door of the tiny house, but no one answered.

"Noah said the kid who built it, Omer, is nice. He gives people tours of the tiny house whenever they ask," Lou explained as they walked around to try knocking on the door of the big house. "This is his sister's place, apparently."

Willow rapped her knuckles against the door. When there was no answer, she pressed the doorbell.

"They might all be at work," Lou whispered, recognizing the fault in their plan. Just because she wasn't at work didn't mean everyone else was home.

Right when they were about to give up hope, the front door swung open. A tall man, around Lou's age, stood in the doorway. He blinked in confusion as he looked at Lou, then Willow. A pudgy beagle came waddling toward the open door. It let out a spirited "Awwoooo" before flopping down into a panting heap at its owner's feet.

Lou stiffened as she noticed a blue dog leash hanging from the coatrack in the entryway. But it was as chunky as one of Willow's halter leads for her horse. This wasn't the thin leash Detective Anderson had been searching for.

Willow's eyes flicked over to it as well. "Is that a horse lead?" she asked with a smirk.

The man's cheeks reddened. "It is." He rubbed at the back of his neck. "Lucy's a puller when we try to walk her, so we need all the help we can get." He motioned to the dog. "Which is why we don't walk her as much as we should," he admitted. "What can I do for you?" he asked.

"We were hoping to talk to someone about the tiny house in the driveway," Willow said. "Is it still for sale?"

Flinching, the man said, "Uh, yeah."

Lou and Willow shared a concerned glance.

"It's my brother-in-law's," the man explained, clearing his throat. "Here, let me get him for you." He bellowed out, "Omer. You've got people here." Turning back to Willow and Lou, he leaned in close. "Sorry in advance if he's a little sour with you. He's still reeling from the news."

"News of what?" Lou asked with concern.

"An inspector came by last week and informed us we don't have the correct permits to keep the tiny home here and for someone to be living in it," the man explained. "He has a month to either get rid of it or pay for the correct permits. If not, he'll get handed a big fine."

"Does he have to get rid of it? Can't he just prove he's not living in there anymore?" Lou knew this wasn't helpful to Willow, but she suddenly wanted to help the young man keep his beloved space.

"He decided to sell it," the man said with a shrug. "Said if he can't live in it, he could at least get some money for it. We're the only people he knows in the area, so he doesn't have anywhere else to put it where he could live inside. The kid had a rough start to life, and he's got a lot of debt. I think it's the right decision, even if it is hard."

Willow shook her head. "I'm so sorry. That's awful."

The man raked a hand through his short-cropped hair. "I know. It's ridiculous." He inhaled like he might say more, but a lanky young man jogged down the stairs. He wore all black and a scowl sharp enough, it looked like it could cut a person. "You've got someone interested in the tiny house."

Omer paused at the bottom of the stairs. Now that they knew the reason he had to sell, it made sense that he would be apprehensive. "Thanks, Terrance. I can take it from here."

Terrance peered down at his brother-in-law, as if he was worried that he couldn't. But then a crashing sound came from the other room, followed by the wail of a young child. Terrance's expression tightened with worry. "I'll leave you to it," he said before turning to jog in that direction. Lucy the beagle waddled after him.

Omer gave a half-hearted wave outside. "Here, let me show you the place."

Lou and Willow followed, feeling awful, like people who were taking someone's beloved pet from them.

Omer turned to face them. "They say it either has to be permitted or I have to pay a fine. And I don't have the money for either. Neither does my sister, not that I want to ask anything more of her. She's already helped me out of enough scrapes."

"Does the county give extensions?" Lou wondered.

Omer's jaw clenched tight before he answered. "Already asked." Omer sighed. "The silly part is that they really don't care all that much, but once they get a complaint, they have to follow protocol."

"Complaint?" Willow asked.

"Someone reported it to the county." Omer nodded slowly. There was a fatigued acceptance in the motion, like he'd already spent all the energy he could being mad about it.

"Do you have any idea who made the complaint?" Lou asked.

A shadow moved behind Omer's eyes, and his gaze flicked across the street. Lou could've sworn Omer looked straight at Nina's house, but he said, "No idea. It's anonymous. Here, let me show you the inside. Sorry, it's a bit of a mess because I'm moving my stuff to *my room* inside the house." The sarcastic way he said *my room* made it seem like it really wasn't.

"You don't want to live in the big house with your family?" Lou asked.

Omer rolled his eyes. He softened for a moment. "Look, I'm grateful to my sister and Terrance for all they've done for me, but I was finally feeling like I had my own space. I had something to be proud of. But they have two little kids, and it's chaotic in there." He gestured to the house. "You heard it. That was tame, and it's all the time." He stuffed his hands in his pockets. "I'm trying to make it work as a freelance graphic designer, and I set my own work hours. When I was out here, I was out of sight, out of mind. Ever since I started moving inside, I'm becoming a babysitter. I pay rent. I'm not trying to get out of pulling my weight. I just wish my weight didn't come in the form of a toddler."

As if he couldn't bear to think about his new situation any longer, Omer unlocked the door to the tiny house and gestured for them to enter. The smell of freshly cut wood stung at Lou's nostrils in the best way possible. The interior was tinier than a house, as the name implied, but more spacious than Lou had been expecting. It was an open design, with a large desk at one end and storage at the other.

"This is my desk area, where I would do my design work." Omer pointed to a space to the right. "Here's the bathroom. It has a composting toilet I used for emergencies, but I'll throw that in for free if you want it."

Willow cut the air with her hand, stopping that line of thinking. "I'm going to make sure there are restrooms on the premises."

Omer gestured to his left where there were cabinets and a sink. "I was still working on all the plumbing to turn this into a small kitchen, so it's basically just cabinets and storage at this point. And here's the built-in couch I was using as a bed."

Willow's eyes were wide with awe. "It's absolutely perfect."

As if he hadn't been looking at everything like it was a small paradise a moment before, he crossed his arms and said, "You know, it's going to take a lot of work to get it plumbed. I basically got as far as insulation and electricity before that busybody turned me in."

Lou's attention, which had been focused on the small fireplace in the corner, snapped back to Omer. "Wait. What busybody? I thought you said you didn't know who it was who reported you?"

Willow lifted an eyebrow. "That's right. You did."

Omer's cheeks turned red, and his eyes jumped around the tiny space, as if looking for an exit. "Uh, I don't. I just assumed it's a busybody since they turned me in," he blurted.

Lou was unconvinced. From the way Willow crossed her arms in front of her chest, she shared in Lou's doubt. Lou wasn't sure if Willow had caught the way he'd glanced over at Nina's house the first time they'd asked him about the person who'd reported him.

But a guy who'd had a rough start, as Terrance had mentioned, and finally felt like he was grasping freedom and what he wanted his life to look like, might snap if the one thing that gave him that freedom was taken away.

"It was Nina, wasn't it?" Lou asked, taking a chance. She had seen no hint of recognition on his face when he'd first seen her, so she didn't think he was her mystery texter, who obviously knew what she looked like.

But that didn't mean he wasn't the killer. Lou still wasn't sure if those two people were different.

Omer's mouth pulled into a tight line, like a string about to snap from intense pressure. "It had to be her. No one else around here was that poisonous." He spat out the words.

"Nina had an excellent reputation in town," Lou blurted before she could think of the consequences.

Omer crossed his arms over his chest. "I was one of the few who knew the truth about who she really was."

"What does that mean?" Willow asked.

The young man was silent for a beat, as if he was considering whether to answer the question. But he sank onto the couch. "I was working on insulation during the summer months, which meant that I didn't have a ton of soundproofing in my house. I heard everything that she did, all the fights she started with people in the neighborhood. That's why she turned me in."

Lou cocked her head. "What do you mean, people in the neighborhood?"

Omer either ignored her question or pretended not to hear her, because he stood and looked at Willow. "Do you have an offer or not?"

Willow blinked, reorienting herself after being pulled from his story about Nina. "Uh..."

"Look, check out my blog." Omer produced a business card and flicked it in her direction. "I catalog how much the supplies cost me. I would at least like to make that money back. If you can add anything more for my labor, that would be great. Come back if you want to make a serious offer." He opened the door and ushered them outside. Before Lou or Willow could say anything more, he disappeared into the big house.

The women stood there for a silent moment.

"Okay then," Willow whispered, turning on her heel and walking in the other direction. "That was enlightening," she said at full volume once they were in the car.

Lou widened her eyes. "Very. I think it's safe to say that Chase wasn't the only one in the neighborhood who hated Nina enough to kill her."

CHAPTER 13

Willow and Lou had only been away from the car for half an hour at the most, but it had been enough time for it to grow chilly inside. Willow turned on the car and set the heater to full blast while they sat there.

"Did you hear what Omer said about other neighbors?" Lou asked. "Do you think he meant Chase, or are there more people angry with Nina, on this street?"

"It's pretty odd that he didn't answer." Willow nodded excitedly. "And that's even without considering all the people Nina may have angered that don't live on this street."

Lou pressed her lips together but didn't say what was on her mind.

Willow glanced back at her, noticing the change. "Oh, but the mystery texter mentioned the killer was a neighbor. Right. I forgot."

"It's okay," Lou said. "My mystery informant could still be the killer, trying to take us in the wrong direction."

"Right," Willow said. "But I can't help but wonder if your

mystery texter isn't being vague because of a different reason, not because they're the killer. The line about not being able to trust their eyes or brain. I'm no expert, but doesn't that kind of sound like someone who might struggle with mental health issues?"

"I wondered the same thing," Lou agreed. "But I'm not an expert either."

"You know who is, though?" Willow asked.

Lou's eyes widened. Of course, it was someone she saw almost daily. "Forrest," she said, naming one of her regulars, a local psychologist. "He won't be able to divulge names of his clients, but he might give us insight into how to get more information out of this person."

"That *would* be a great idea," Willow said pointedly, catching the fact they'd fallen back into sleuthing mode. "*If* we were getting involved."

"Which we're not," Lou agreed.

It was easy when there was information right in front of them, but she'd made a promise to stay out of the case.

Willow peered through the windshield. "Now, where should we go next? Because I think they're going to think we're weird if we sit here any longer."

Lou chuckled, but she had an idea. "What if we try talking to Peggy Lee Milton again?"

Willow's eyes lit up. "Really?"

"She didn't even hear your proposal last time," Lou said. "Let me try talking to her."

People had often told Lou that she had a calming air about her. Maybe she could make a difference by helping turn Willow's dream into a reality. If she could, she wanted to try.

Willow gripped the steering wheel with excitement and started driving in that direction.

If possible, the foliage was even more beautiful than it had been on Tuesday. Willow wound through the farmland roads as they left Lakeside County and ventured up into Skagit County. During the summer, the valley's tulips were the stars, luring thousands of tourists, with their vibrant colors. But the rich auburns, mustards, and tones of burnt Sienna felt just as impressive to Lou.

They pulled up to Milton Farm just as they had the first time, but both women got out of the car this time.

Peggy Lee Milton was waiting for them by the time they reached her front porch. She was sitting on the porch swing, lazily moving back and forth. She chewed on sunflower seeds like she was at a baseball game and wore a thick flannel with old denim overalls. Her gray hair was short and unkempt, like it hadn't seen a brush in a while. For a second, it almost seemed as if she might be relaxing.

Until Lou got a good look at her face.

It was wrinkled into the most intense scowl Lou had ever seen.

"You brought backup this time." Peggy Lee growled out the words.

Despite every instinct Lou had to run, she and Willow kept climbing the porch steps until they stood at the top and faced the woman on the swing. Lou searched the space, hoping Peggy Lee didn't have a shotgun stored somewhere to use when her glower didn't effectively scare off visitors.

"Mrs. Milton," Willow started. "I'm really sorry to bother you again, but you didn't give me a chance to tell you why I stopped by last time." Willow pushed back her shoulders, so she stood her full six feet.

Peggy Lee spat sunflower seed husks onto the porch a little too close to their feet for Lou's comfort. "That's because I don't want to hear what you have to say. Whatever comes out of that mouth of yours isn't going to do anything but bug me. I'm not selling anything I have. I don't want to buy anything you have. All I want is to be left alone, in peace," she finished, spitting again, this time the seed shell hit a little closer to Willow's foot.

Willow pressed her lips together.

"'I go among trees and sit still. All my stirring becomes quiet around me like circles on water,'" Lou said.

"What was that, little one?" Peggy Lee peered at Lou. The way she said little one wasn't at all endearing or a compliment. She let out a husky laugh. "I'm sorry. I'm sure you're a normal-sized woman. It's just next to this lanky string bean, you're like a miniature."

Willow grumbled something to herself, but Lou ignored her and stepped closer to the older woman on the swing, careful not to step on the discarded seed shells.

"It's a line from Wendell Berry. I think you'd like his writing. My husband used to teach English, and he did an entire unit on agricultural writers. This farmhouse, this land, reminds me of the romanticism in their writing." Lou tried to stay calm even though each word she said seemed to spin Peggy Lee even further into a mad rage.

By the time Lou finished speaking, Peggy Lee was almost red in the face. "Your husband used to teach? Huh?" She spat out the words as intensely as she had with the seeds. "What is he now, unemployed?" She chuckled at what she seemed to think was a joke.

"He passed away last year," Lou whispered.

Peggy Lee's smirk dropped.

Willow stepped forward. "Peggy Lee, you and Lou have so much—" She sucked in a breath as she stopped herself. "Never mind. Sorry, I shouldn't have brought it up."

Peggy Lee clenched her jaw, looking somehow even angrier that Willow wouldn't finish her thought.

Lou knew where she'd been going. "What she meant to say is we have a lot in common. We both recently lost our husbands. They were both named Benjamin, actually."

"I was wrong to bring it up." Willow shook her head.

Lou grabbed her friend's hand. "It's okay."

They turned their attention to Peggy Lee. But instead of softening like Willow had probably expected after hearing the similarities, Peggy Lee burst forward out of the swing like a rabid wolverine. She snarled; her face contorted into so much rage, Lou was sure the woman was in physical pain, not just emotional.

"No, she really shouldn't have brought it up. And the day before the anniversary of Benji's death, no less." Peggy Lee showed Willow her teeth. "How dare you? This is a hard enough week as it is."

"We didn't know. I didn't mean to make it harder," Willow said. "I want to talk to you about renting your land, growing things on it again, just like you and Benji used to!" Willow spat out the sentences as if they were threats instead of requests.

Lou took a step back. These two stubborn women were too much alike. This would not end well. She'd been wrong to suggest they try again. Hooking her arm through her friend's, Lou pulled Willow back.

"I think it's time to go. She doesn't want to talk with us," Lou pleaded.

There was a moment where Willow pulled in a deep breath like she was going to try again, but then she turned to follow Lou off the porch.

"That's right. Leave me in peace!" Peggy Lee shouted after them.

"Peace?" Willow said over her shoulder. "The only thing you're living in is misery and anger."

The sound of a seed being spat and ricocheting off the porch followed. Lou flinched as it hit her in the back.

Willow hunched over the steering wheel after they'd piled back into her car. "That woman is certifiably difficult."

Lou wrinkled her nose. "If I didn't have you, maybe that's what I would be like four years from now."

Willow rolled her eyes as she turned to face Lou. "You could never become like that cranky mess."

Shrugging, Lou said, "I don't know. If you hadn't helped pull me out of my depression after Ben passed, maybe I would. It sounds like she was lucky enough to love her husband more than anything else in this world." Lou swallowed, and then started again, overcome by the emotion, knowing what that was like—how wonderful and terrible it could be. "She just didn't have a best friend to catch her when she fell, because her only best friend was gone."

Willow puffed out her cheeks. "Well, when you put it that way, now I feel bad for her."

"Don't feel bad," Lou said. "Just understand that she's not in a place to give you what you want, and that's okay. I'll help you find somewhere else. There are tons of farms around here. Maybe someone else wants to lease out their land."

Willow placed a hand on Lou's. "Thank you. You're a good friend."

Lou embraced the light feeling that spread through her chest at her friend's words. "Back atcha. Now let's drive around and find you the perfect land, okay?"

They spent the rest of the afternoon driving around the area, stopping by small mom-and-pop stores and feedstores to put out the word that Willow was hoping to rent some land for a nursery. They had a few promising leads by the time they drove home to Button that afternoon.

"Good day off?" Willow asked as she let Lou out in front of the bookshop.

Lou nodded once. "Great day off. Thank you for convincing me I needed it."

"I'm always here to play hooky from work until I've got a business to run too." Willow's lips arched into a teasing grin. "Then I'll probably be crazy like you and rarely take a day off."

Lou loved how Willow practically shone each time she talked about her nursery. It really was her life's passion, and Lou was so glad she could be here to support her friend in making her dream become a reality.

They said goodbye, and Lou let herself inside. There were still a few hours left until the bookshop would usually be closed for the day, so she left the sign up on the door. Padding up the stairs and into her apartment, Lou greeted the cats as they swarmed around her, ready for a snack. She fed them, sitting back and lacing her fingers behind her head contentedly as she watched them eat, purring as they licked their dishes clean.

But as happy as Lou was to be back in her apartment, her thoughts were again with Peggy Lee on Milton Farm. What Lou had told Willow was truer than her best friend knew. It had been part of the reason Lou had made the move three thousand miles across the country to live in Button, next to Willow.

She'd been spiraling, and a future like Peggy Lee's had been her trajectory.

Lou hadn't been alone on a farm in the middle of a beautiful valley, but being in New York City, surrounded by people, often felt just as lonely. In the months following Ben's death—once family and friends left the city, the funeral was over, and people stopped checking in on her all the time—Lou had scared herself.

She'd stopped running or reading for fun and got most of her food delivered. Thinking about cooking in their kitchen alone was too hard. They would never cook another meal together, dancing through the kitchen as they chatted, cooked, and sipped on wine. They would never run through Central Park together again or discuss a book they'd read together.

Lou had eventually gone back to work at the publishing house where she was an editor, but she worked from home on projects more often than not, only going into the office when she had a meeting or needed to see a client.

Ben had always been the outgoing one in the relationship. He got her out on the town, convinced her to go on vacations, even knew when she just needed a walk in the fresh air. Like Willow, Ben had been Lou's perfect complement. Without him, she had begun shrinking into a life she didn't recognize.

She'd known she couldn't keep going like that, and she'd known she needed to get away. It was on one of her worst days, when Lou hadn't been able to change out of her pajamas, had called in sick to work, and couldn't seem to get out of bed, that Willow had called with news of the bookshop for sale in Button, Washington.

Lou knew it was Ben, saving her again, bringing her to Willow: the one person he knew who could help. As grateful as Lou was for that, her heart hurt thinking about Peggy Lee. The woman obviously didn't have anyone like that.

Lou made a decision. She said goodbye to the cats, grabbed her purse, and jogged out to her car.

CHAPTER 14

Less than an hour later, Lou was heading back to Milton Farm. This time, it was just her in the car. Well, she was accompanied by a basket, sitting buckled into her passenger seat.

She'd had momentary flashbacks of the apology basket she'd brought to Nina on Monday and wondered if this time would go just as poorly, but she pushed those worries out of her mind and drove.

This was a care basket, not an apology basket. It included fresh flowers from the local florist, a few of Lou's favorites from the Button Bakery, and a card. Inside the card, Lou had simply written:

Peggy Lee,

Thinking of you on this difficult anniversary. I'm only just past one year, but I can imagine five is going to be just as hard (and ten and fifteen, and so on). If you ever need to chat, I'm here (no pressure to talk about the farm).

Lou

She'd left her phone number on the bottom. As she pulled

up to the Milton farmhouse, Lou could see the porch swing was empty. She was happy to see that, though it seemed like a bit of a shame since the setting sun was throwing beautiful colors across the crisp autumn sky, and the porch overlooking the farmland seemed like the perfect, peaceful place to watch.

Tiptoeing up the steps, Lou set the basket on the porch, shoved it a foot closer to the door, and then pivoted. She jogged back down the steps, waiting to celebrate her sneakiness until she was just a little farther away.

She had cleared the last step when the creak of the front door sounded behind her. Lou froze but couldn't seem to convince her body to turn around. She curled her shoulders forward and hunched her back in preparation for being hit with a seed shell or vegetables.

But neither happened.

The creak of an old board moaned behind her. Lou winced and turned around. Peggy Lee stood on the porch, staring down at the basket. Tears streamed down her face.

"Is this to bribe me?" she asked as angrily as anyone could while they were actively crying. She swiped at her cheeks. "Because I'm having a bad day already, and I will not let you make it worse."

Lou studied her shoes for a moment. "You said it's the fifth anniversary tomorrow. I just brought you that to help, if just a little." She took a step back to show her she wasn't a threat. She wasn't trying to stay and talk.

Peggy Lee's eyes snapped up, but her expression softened. "Thank you," she whispered.

Lou smiled and nodded, then she took another slow step backward. "I'll leave you alone now. I'm sorry."

To Lou's surprise, Peggy Lee held up a hand, palm flat. She glared at it, dropping it back by her side like it had betrayed her, but then she said, "Do you want to come inside?"

Lou's lungs burned with the emotions of the moment, and she found it hard to breathe, or speak, so she simply walked forward. Warmth wrapped around Lou as she stepped inside the farmhouse. A fire crackled in a large stone hearth in the middle of the space.

The interior was rustic, worn, and crowded with knick-knacks, but homey at the same time. Scents of pine and cinnamon permeated the space.

Peggy Lee gestured for Lou to have a seat on a worn leather couch. "Can I get you some tea?" she asked.

Not only did Lou want tea, but she also had a feeling that the job was important in that moment for Peggy Lee.

"I would love some. Thank you." Lou folded her hands in her lap.

Peggy Lee walked down a short hallway into what Lou assumed was the kitchen. While she was alone, Lou took in the details of the home. Old farming equipment hung on the walls as decoration instead of functional pieces. Pictures of Peggy Lee with her husband littered the space. Lou couldn't help but notice how much happier Peggy Lee looked in the photographs. She was still rough around the edges, wearing those same worn overalls in many of the pictures, but there was a wide grin on her face.

Peggy Lee returned a few minutes later with a tray laden with a full tea set. It was a beautiful porcelain set with a rhodo-dendron pattern painted on its delicate surfaces and gold leaf accents. Lou didn't mean to stare, but a set like that was built for entertaining company, and it seemed an odd choice for someone who Willow had deemed antisocial at the best of times.

Peggy Lee must've understood Lou's internal question, because she said, "Benji loved to have company. He took after his mother in that way. This set was hers before she passed."

"It's gorgeous." Lou admired the hand-painted flowers and the vibrant teal background. When she glanced up from the tea set, Peggy Lee was scrutinizing her with the same intensity that Lou had used while studying the tea set.

"Can I ask how your husband passed?" Peggy Lee asked. Her voice was a whisper of itself, but her signature gruffness was still present.

Lou's gaze dropped to her hands. "Heart attack. No family history. He was healthy. Just like that, he was gone." Lou's eyes watered, and she found Peggy Lee in the same state when she looked up again. "What about your Benjamin?"

Sniffing, Peggy Lee said, "Stomach cancer. That man rarely got sick, and he went to the doctor even less." She let out a nostalgic laugh. "But one day he started complaining of a stomachache. I knew it was bad when he asked me to drive him to the doctor. He was gone less than a month later." Peggy Lee closed her watery eyes and shook her head as if she still couldn't believe it.

Lou knew that feeling all too well.

Peggy Lee mumbled something about the tea being ready, so she began pouring it into the waiting teacups. She held one toward Lou.

"I'm so sorry." Lou took the proffered teacup, holding up a hand when Peggy Lee gestured to sugar and milk. "I don't prefer any in my tea, thank you." She took her first sip.

The tea was a spiced blend that made Lou feel like she was wrapped up in a blanket of all the best Thanksgiving spices.

"It's hard to find people who understand," Peggy Lee said after a beat of silence.

Lou nodded, giving Peggy Lee space to say more if she wanted.

"Friends never seemed like a necessity to me. I had Benji. He was my best friend." Peggy Lee let her finger trail over the lip of the teacup. "Then, when he was gone, the few acquaintances I had couldn't handle my grief, nor should I have expected them to. I didn't make them a priority when they needed me, only when I needed them. It's better this way, though. Fewer people to disappoint." She glanced up at Lou as if she knew what she'd just said was wrong, and she was waiting to see if Lou called her on it.

Taking a fortifying breath, Lou weighed her words carefully. "Everyone's entitled to their own grieving process."

"But you would've done things differently?" Peggy Lee read into what Lou wasn't saying.

Lou shrugged. "Probably not. I had plenty of friends and acquaintances who stopped talking to me after Ben died. They didn't know what to say or weren't able to support me on my healing journey. Like you, I understood why they couldn't be there. The only difference with me is that I had Willow, the woman who was with me earlier."

At the mention of Lou's best friend, Peggy Lee's face tightened back up again.

"She's the only reason I didn't close myself off, shut myself in," Lou said truthfully. "She never gave up on me, even though I gave her plenty of opportunities."

Peggy Lee huffed. "What does she *really* want with my land?"

Lou held up a hand. "Oh no. That's not why I'm here. I promise. We won't bother you about the land anymore. It was an idea that she realizes can't happen. She'll adapt."

"I would've expected more persistence from such a seemingly stubborn person." Peggy Lee cocked her eyebrow in an expression that almost looked disappointed.

Lou chuckled. "I convinced her there were other options. Without me, I think you would've been seeing her every day for the foreseeable future."

Peggy Lee sipped her tea as she contemplated that. "What does she want to grow?"

Careful not to let her excitement show too much, Lou said, "It's always been her dream to own a nursery. She's got a spot rented in downtown Button for the sales portion but doesn't want to buy from the big suppliers. She wants to grow everything herself."

"She's right to," Peggy Lee said. "Some of those suppliers are fine, but we had clients who said they sold them diseased plants. Even if they're healthy, often they don't survive the long treks they have to make across state lines because they're fragile and aren't native to the area."

"Exactly her thoughts. But while she's found a couple larger plots of land, she says there's no parcel that has soil as good as you have on your farm." Lou found herself getting too far into flattery, and she didn't want to scare off Peggy Lee when she'd only just gotten her to listen. "Willow would do all the work on the land. You wouldn't have to do anything," Lou promised.

"Well..." Peggy Lee's nose twitched. "I *could* use the income. Benji's life insurance paid off what we still owed on the land and the house, but I'm going to have to get a job to pay for the rest of life."

The woman was likely in her fifties, so she had at least ten years until she could retire, Lou guessed, not knowing what their retirement savings looked like.

Peggy Lee nodded once. "Tell her she's got a deal. She's gotta show me a detailed plan of what she wants to do to the land, but after that, I'll draw up a rental agreement. The greenhouses will need some TLC, but I'd say they're still usable."

Lou's heart soared. "Peggy Lee, that's... Thank you. You won't regret it."

"I'd better not." She narrowed her eyes at Lou, but then broke into a gruff laugh. "Now, should we break into those baked items you brought?"

Lou felt the weight of at least one of her worries lift off her shoulders. "Definitely."

They walked into the kitchen. The space matched the rest of the house, rustic and homey. The cabinets were painted a sage-green color that immediately made Lou feel relaxed, and the countertops were made from butcher block. Shelves held beautiful sets of what appeared to be handcrafted pottery bowls, plates, and tumblers.

Peggy Lee noticed Lou admiring them. "My neighbor is a potter. I have a hard time staying away when she has a kiln opening, as you can see."

Lou was sure she would have to work hard to say no to beautiful pieces like that as well.

Peggy Lee plucked the bakery box from the basket and twiddled her fingers as she opened it. But Lou's attention caught on a stainless-steel water bowl that sat empty on the tile floor in the corner of the room.

"Do you have a pet?" Lou asked, pointing to the water bowl. She hadn't seen a dog or cat.

"Not anymore." Peggy Lee stared at the bowl. "Benji and I had a dog years ago, but he was old and passed away about six years ago. We had talked about getting another one, and then I lost Benji, and I couldn't wrap my head around raising a puppy on my own. It was a lot of work when it was the two of us." She puffed out her cheeks. "But I keep that bowl there to remind myself that someday, I'd like a companion again."

"Have you thought of adopting an older dog?" Lou offered, thinking of Mr. Muffins. As soon as she mentioned it, she remembered how much care that particular dog needed, and realized he might not be the best fit for Peggy Lee, so she added, "Or a cat? They take significantly less training than a dog."

Peggy Lee snorted. "Yeah, because you can't train 'em." Despite her comment, she tipped her head to the side. "I hadn't thought about a cat."

Lou tried to keep her excitement in check. "I own a bookstore that doubles as a rescue-cat sanctuary. You would be welcome anytime if you want to meet the adoptable cats."

Chewing on her lip, Peggy Lee frowned. "I'm outside so much, though. I wonder if that would be fair to a cat who's stuck inside all day."

Perking up, Lou thought about Holden Clawfield and his intense love of the outdoors. He would need someone who could watch over him and make sure he didn't get into trouble outside.

Lou grinned. "I think I might have just the perfect cat for you."

CHAPTER 15

Lou was too excited to wait until she got home to call Willow, so she called her from the car as she pulled out from Peggy Lee's driveway.

"Guess what?" she said when Willow answered the call.

"What?" Willow asked, following directions. "Why does it sound like you're driving?"

"Because I am." Lou pulled out of the long driveway at Milton Farm. "It turns out you were right about Peggy Lee."

"What do you mean?" The hope in Willow's voice would've destroyed Lou if she'd been in the possession of any less exciting news.

"Well, I went back. It was only to bring Peggy Lee a care basket for the fifth anniversary of Benji's death tomorrow, but she invited me inside, and we got to talking." Lou didn't want to leave Willow hanging for too long, so she continued with her story. "At first, we were just talking about our Benjamins, but after a while she asked me about you and what you wanted with her land. I told her the truth, and she said she'll talk to you."

Willow let out an excited squeal on the other end of the call. "That's amazing!"

"She wants you to submit a plan for how you want to use the land. But after that, she'll draw up a rental agreement," Lou added quickly so Willow had all the facts before she truly started celebrating.

"Sure. Absolutely." Lou could picture Willow nodding as she said this. "I can start on that right away. Oh, Lou, you have no idea how much this means to me."

"I think I do." She chuckled. "But honestly, it wasn't anything I did. I just told her the truth about the person you are and the great things you want to do with this nursery."

Willow scoffed. "It was *everything* that you did. Don't be modest. I knew that you would have the calm energy to explain to her that this will be such a good thing for both of us."

"I really think it will," Lou said. "She talked about money being an issue. You paying her rent for the land will afford her the financial comfort she needs."

"For sure," Willow agreed. "Oh, speaking of financial comfort, I consulted Omer's blog and his list of expenses for the tiny house. I can afford to pay him a fair amount for his labor and still be well within my budget for building structures for the nursery."

"That's great," Lou said. "I'll add one more thing to the list of good news. Peggy Lee was talking about pets and wanting a companion again, and I suggested she meet Holden Clawfield since he seems like the perfect outdoor farm kitty. She wants to meet him as soon as possible."

"I'm so happy for him and for her—you too. Now you won't have to act like a linebacker blocking the door every time someone comes or goes." Willow chortled.

Lou did too. The relief was tremendous. "Okay, well, I'm

going to call Noah while I'm driving back and see if he can give me any insight on Peggy Lee as a pet owner. I want to get her paperwork going as soon as possible, so I can get him in a place where he doesn't feel like he's imprisoned."

"Gotcha. I'll let you go, then," Willow said. "Thank you, again."

"Anytime."

They hung up, and Lou immediately called Noah. He didn't pick up, which wasn't surprising since the clinic wasn't quite closed yet, but she left a message letting him know she had a few questions and to call her back when he had a chance.

The rest of the drive back, Lou let herself sink into her driver's seat, take it slow, and appreciate the beautiful fall foliage for yet another time that week.

By the time she pulled her car into the parking space in the alley behind her bookstore, she was feeling relaxed. Everything was coming together. She walked into the bookshop through the back door, remembering the sign on the front door. She went to peel the taped sign off the glass.

But as she walked toward the front of the building, she noticed something that hadn't been there before.

Lou raced out onto the sidewalk in front of the shop and stared in awe at two beautiful potted Japanese maple trees that now flanked her shop windows. Their leaves looked like they were on fire, just like the ones she'd been appreciating on her drive home.

She pulled out her phone and called Willow.

"Hello?" Willow answered in her most coy tone, the one that told Lou she was smiling mischievously.

"I thought you were going to get right to work on that proposal for Peggy Lee?" Lou asked.

Willow sucked in a breath through her teeth. "Yes, but I just potted these beautiful maples today, and they were calling your name. I wanted to say thank you. So, thank you."

Happy tears gathered in the corners of Lou's eyes. "Thank you. They're gorgeous. When you open your nursery, we're going to have to put little signs on them, telling people where they came from and where they can find their own."

"Girl, when I open my nursery, you're going to have seasonal plants in front of your shop all the time. But yes, signage is a good idea." Willow sounded thoughtful. "Okay, *now* I'm off to work on that proposal."

"Good luck." Lou ended the call and gave the maples one last glance of appreciation before she went inside.

Before she could close the door behind her, Lou heard someone calling her name. She poked her head back out the shop door and saw Noah jogging down the street toward her.

"Hey, I just closed up. I got your message and figured I'd swing by." He stopped and eyed the trees. "These are great. Willow?"

"Of course." Lou beckoned him inside, pulling the sign from the window.

He noticed and asked, "You closed today? Is everything okay?"

"It is now," she said. "The incident yesterday at the corn maze left me a little creeped out, and Willow convinced me to take a mental health day. I'm feeling much better now."

Noah gave her a supportive nod. "I'm glad. What was it you wanted to ask me?"

At this, Lou perked up. "I have a potential adopter for Holden Clawfield, but I wanted to run the name by you in case you have any background with them."

Lou explained how she and Willow had been talking to

Peggy Lee about her land and how the woman had mentioned wanting another pet.

"Did you ever treat the dog they had, or did they take it to someone else?" Lou asked, hopeful Noah would have good information to share with her.

"Bentley," Noah said. "He was a Border collie. They took great care of that dog." He tipped his head to one side. "I can't say for sure since it was Benji and Peggy Lee taking care of the dog together. Sometimes there's one person in the relationship who's better at keeping up with an animal's care than the other, but I would trust her with a pet. I would say we should just ask a few questions about cat ownership and what having a hybrid indoor-outdoor cat means to her. I'd be happy to come with you for the drop-off if you'd like."

Lou pressed her hands together. "That would be amazing. I'm free any afternoon coming up. Just let me know what works for you."

He pulled out his phone. "How does tomorrow, after you close, sound?"

"Perfect." Saturdays were busy for Lou at the bookshop, but Noah's clinic was closed on the weekends. He usually kept busy with handyman work around town or helping at his family's quilt shop. Sometimes she wondered when he had time to relax.

Lou was about to put the laminated sign from the window in a drawer, when she remembered she needed to look up the person who'd called her that time about his book order.

"Can't forget that," she whispered to herself because, in all the hubbub of the day, she had almost let it slip her mind.

"What?" Noah asked, having heard what she'd only meant for herself.

"I was just reminding myself about something." She waved

at the sign, but Noah gave her such an interested look that she filled him in. "It's just, you know my mystery texter?"

He nodded warily, obviously having very different feelings about the person after what had transpired in the corn maze.

"I was wondering how they got my personal number, but then I remembered I used to hang this up each Monday and Tuesday, back when I was trying out the whole closing-early thing, before I officially changed my store hours." She pointed to the number at the bottom.

Noah made a deep humming noise as he contemplated that news. "And anyone walking by could've written it down or entered it into their phone."

"Exactly," Lou said.

"So what aren't you supposed to forget? Changing it to your shop phone?" he asked.

"Actually, a customer did contact me with a book emergency early in the summer. He wanted to cancel an expensive order and wanted to try to catch me before I went through with the order. I was going to look into the person to see if that gave me any clues. While someone could've taken a picture or written it down, it seems even more likely that they had it saved on their phone, if they called me once."

"Good call." Noah stepped closer as Lou went over to her computer and woke it up from its sleepy day off.

Going back through her sales records, she found her canceled orders and pulled up the correct one.

"It's a Jonah Frazier," Lou said, feeling like that name sounded familiar.

"Whoa," Noah said.

"What?" Lou asked, glancing over her shoulder to gauge his reaction.

"That's Nina's backyard neighbor," Noah said. His gaze

flicked around the room as he seemed to get all his thoughts in line.

She opened her hands, palms up. "That has to be him, then. He must be my mystery texter. Jonah Frazier obviously saw something from his window and is trying to lead me to the killer. It's not the killer, after all." Lou felt like celebrating.

But Noah shook his head.

"Why?" Lou asked, incredulous. "Noah, this makes so much sense."

"It does, all except one big hitch. Jonah Frazier was sentenced to twenty years in prison. He's been locked up for the past three months."

CHAPTER 16

Lou paced through the bookshop. The startling news Noah had just dropped on her about Jonah Frazier took her brain a moment to digest.

"That means..." she mumbled to herself as her brain tried to make the puzzle piece fit.

"Nothing," Noah said, answering the question for her. "It must've been someone else who saw your sign and copied your number. They charged Jonah with robbing a jewelry store. His incarceration has nothing to do with Nina. There's also no way he could be Nina's killer or your mystery texter."

Lou nodded slowly as she realized the same truths. The puzzle piece had fooled her. It seemed to be the right one, but no matter how hard she tried to shove it into place, it didn't fit.

Her shoulders slumped forward. "I guess I got excited over nothing."

Noah shot her a dimpled smile. "Happens to the best of us." He drummed his fingers on the counter. "You'll call me when you're ready to go tomorrow?"

"I will." Lou waved goodbye to Noah as he headed out into

the foggy fall evening. Lou locked the door behind her. She shut down her shop computer and ambled upstairs. The cats were all asleep, napping in various places around her apartment. She curled up with Sapphire on her couch, pulling a fuzzy blanket over her lap and grabbing her laptop instead of a book.

Lou felt like a kid trying to get away with something she wasn't supposed to be doing. She'd decided not to get involved in this case anymore. But she'd been unable to stop herself from questioning Omer earlier and couldn't help but obsess over what she'd just learned about Jonah Frazier. Omer had mentioned that he wasn't the only neighbor Nina had negatively impacted.

What if Noah was wrong, and Nina somehow had a hand in Jonah's incarceration? Lou's mind wouldn't be able to rest until she knew for sure.

She pulled up the Lakeside County website on her laptop and began searching recent cases in the county court system. It didn't take her long to find Jonah Frazier's. She read through the public transcript information about the crimes they charged Jonah with, knowing it would only be a snapshot, but hoping it might give her enough to connect the two.

Her mind easily wove a story about the troubled young man robbing the jewelry store, thinking he'd gotten away with it, only to have his nosy neighbor call the police, letting them know she'd seen him with the jewels.

Lou's eyes pored over the page. The robbery had happened five months prior. It had taken place in the middle of the night. What if Nina had been outside with Mr. Muffins, on one of his many bathroom trips when she'd seen Jonah coming home from the robbery? He might be stuck in prison, but it wasn't out of the question for him to hire a friend or colleague to kill her for him.

Lou wrinkled her nose at that thought. Maybe she'd been reading too many thrillers lately. Her mind couldn't help but dive right into the ruthless-killer plotline. She decided she needed more facts instead of wild hunches that belonged in fiction. Turning back to the screen, she skipped other court documents to open the one that held the final verdict for the case.

But as Lou read further, she realized Nina couldn't have been involved. The security cameras had caught Jonah's license plate, and the police had tracked him down the next day. There hadn't been any tips from Button residents. She didn't see Nina Upton anywhere as an eyewitness. There weren't even anonymous eyewitnesses. They had only needed the camera footage.

Lou huffed out a frustrated sigh as she read the very bottom line on the page, where the judge signed off on the verdict. Judge Craig Potts had tried the case—the recently killed Judge Potts. She thought of Easton's investigation, how few leads he seemed to have, and the intense local pressure on him to solve the case as quickly as possible.

Clicking back to the page with the case lists, Lou used the search function at the top of the screen to narrow the list down to mentions of Nina Upton.

Four cases were listed on the screen.

The first was from almost ten years ago. Nina had sued a man for damages after he rear-ended her car. Writing his name on her list, Lou moved on to the next suit. That one was from two years ago. Nina was the plaintiff, again. She sued a woman named Megan Clark, who owned a business called Button Gifts, a shop that no longer existed, to Lou's knowledge. Nina had, apparently, tripped on uneven concrete outside Megan's business, resulting in a compound fracture.

Lou wasn't sure if Megan's gift shop had gone out of business because of this lawsuit or something else, but the possibility that it had been Nina's lawsuit that bankrupted Button Gifts was too chilling not to consider. Lou shivered at the thought that it could've been her in that situation had Sapphire done any more damage to her arm—or if Nina hadn't died the next day.

Again, she wrote the name on her list and moved on. Cases from years prior wouldn't necessarily be great motives for murder unless there had been recent developments.

The third case on file was Nina's suit against Chase Humphrey for the fence, with documentation about when she reopened the suit after the fence was rebuilt.

But a final case had been filed just a few weeks ago. In fact, there wasn't even a verdict. The suit was still in discovery. Nina was the plaintiff, again. She was suing someone named Devon Goddard for damages after eating food from his food truck, Grown Up Grilled Cheese, which allegedly gave her food poisoning. She'd missed a cruise she had booked that week because she was feeling so poorly. She was suing for the thousands of dollars she lost on the cruise tickets since she didn't have travel insurance, and they wouldn't refund her money last minute.

Lou chewed on her lip as she read. She opened a new tab and typed in Grown Up Grilled Cheese and pulled up the website. While the food truck was available for catering upon request, its normal location was in the parking lot of a gas station ten minutes northwest of Button. The reviews were fantastic.

A few thousand dollars didn't seem like something worth killing over, but if it got out that Devon's food gave people food poisoning, it could damage his excellent reputation. That might be something, especially if the truck was his only means of income.

His hours showed he served lunch and dinner, so he was probably open now. But it wasn't like Lou was going to go. She wasn't supposed to be doing any investigating, let alone going by herself to question possible suspects.

She closed her laptop and appraised her apartment. The sun had set, leaving only the glow from the streetlights outside and the one small light over her oven. It was time for dinner, and she really should relax during the rest of her day off. She could decide what she was going to do with the information she'd learned tomorrow.

Lou reheated some leftovers and curled onto the couch. But instead of reaching for the intense thriller she'd been reading, full of drug lords who hired hits from prison, she pulled a light romantic comedy off her to-be-read pile and started that as she ate.

THE NEXT MORNING, Lou's regulars filed into the bookshop as usual. But unlike their normal quiet routine, they chattered at Lou, wondering why she'd been closed the day prior.

"Is everything okay?" George asked, concern marring her normally easygoing expression as she flopped onto the floor and greeted Anne Mice and Holden Clawfield.

"We were worried," Forrest said, exuding his usual calm tone.

"Would've been nice to have a heads-up," Silas grumbled.

Lou chuckled. "I'm fine. I just needed a mental health day. Willow convinced me."

"And I'll do it again if you don't stop making her feel bad

about it," Willow said, entering the bookshop. Her leg shot out to the right at just the perfect moment to stop Holden from darting through the small gap as the door closed behind her. "No you don't, little one," she said.

"Hopefully today will be the last day I have to worry about him getting out," Lou said.

"You found a place for him?" George asked sadly.

Lou nodded. "He needs a home where he can be outside for at least part of the time. He's going stir crazy here. I think I've found the perfect spot for you, though, Holden," she told the little cream cat as he blinked up at her.

"With whom?" Forrest asked.

Lou checked with Willow first, knowing the explanation involved Willow's business.

"Peggy Lee Milton," Willow said. "I'm going to be renting out her land for the nursery."

"You got Peggy Lee to rent her land to you?" Silas asked dubiously.

Willow beamed. "Lou did."

Forrest nodded as if it didn't surprise him in the least. "I always thought she just needed a friend. I think you'll be good for her."

"Poor Peggy Lee," George said, clicking her tongue. "A few of my friends worked for the farm back in high school. They really liked Benji. Peggy Lee has always been prickly, but she got so much worse after Benji died."

"She's hurting, that's for sure," Lou said. "But Willow's going to give her some income, and hopefully Holden will be the perfect company."

George had to go, and Willow was about to follow when Lou stopped her.

"Noah and I are taking Holden out to Peggy Lee today, if you want to tag along. I don't know if you have your proposal written up yet, but I thought I'd offer," she said.

Willow's eyes lit up. "I just finished it this morning. That sounds great."

Once Willow left, Lou wandered over to where Forrest sat, reading. The adorable Anne Mice had curled up in his lap. Try as she might, Lou couldn't seem to drop the case, which meant she needed an expert opinion about her mystery texter.

Forrest looked up from his book, setting it aside once Lou took a seat in the chair next to him.

"I have an odd question for you about mental health," Lou started, not sure how else to break into the questions she had for him.

"Those are my favorite kind." Forrest smiled calmly, petting Anne Mice as he waited.

Lou shifted in her seat as she thought about how to word her query. "Okay, well, if someone you were talking to seemed a little paranoid and mentioned that they couldn't trust their eyes or their brain, what would you make of that? Would you think they're mentally unstable and not to be trusted?"

Forrest considered her words for a moment. "There are many variables that can lead to paranoia. But the part about not trusting their eyes or their mind interests me the most. Sure, you could be talking with someone who has schizophrenia or another mental ailment that includes hallucinations. You could just as easily be talking to someone who's been brainwashed into believing what they think or see is not valid. There's also medication and its side effects to consider. Those can often mess with a person's perception."

Lou nodded along as Forrest talked, but she didn't feel like she was getting the definite answer to her question that she'd been looking for.

"Long answer short, I can't tell you whether to trust this person. Only you can decide that." Forrest tilted his head apologetically, knowing that wasn't what Lou wanted to hear.

She wrinkled her nose. "That's the problem, Forrest. I don't know that I can." And if she made the wrong decision, the consequence could be deadly.

CHAPTER 17

Noah showed up a few minutes before Willow that evening. Lou stood out front of the bookshop, Holden sitting quiet and happy in the cat carrier at her feet. He was silent, happy being outside in the fresh air. His pink nose pressed up against the metal door as he sniffed the crisp, fall air.

"Evening, you two." Noah stooped to say hello to Holden. "How'd the shop do today?" he asked Lou once he was back on her level.

"Good, once everyone got over the surprise that I closed on Friday." Lou chuckled. "That'll show me to make a last-minute decision to close the bookshop again."

She joked, but Lou really loved how much her bookshop full of cats had become a solace for the people of Button and tourists alike. Not only did she have repeat tourism, but new customers came in all the time saying they'd heard about her shop from a friend.

"Mr. Muffins still doing well?" Lou asked

"He is. I think Kathy's patience might be running a little

thin, but I've got a few feelers out for at least a foster home for him."

"Oh, good." Lou hoped one of them would work out. He was a sweet dog.

Willow pulled up, screeching to a stop. She fought with a pile of papers and folders on the front seat before Lou and Noah got inside. Noah took Holden's crate and climbed in the back, motioning to Lou to sit up front with Willow. He gave her a worried look, one that Lou shared. Willow's hair was coming loose from the bun she'd gathered it into, appearing just as frazzled as she seemed.

"Honest three," Lou said as she buckled in.

It was the way they checked in with each other. The rule was that the person being asked had to answer the first three emotions they were feeling.

"Excited. Terrified. Doubtful." Willow's nostrils flared as she said the last one.

"Like you think it won't happen?" Noah asked.

"Yeah," Willow admitted. "I feel like I'm going to get to the top step on her porch, and she's going to have a bunch of vegetables to throw at me again while she laughs."

"The meeting I had with Peggy Lee and the one Willow had were very different," Lou explained to Noah. "I can see why she thinks that."

Lou stopped there, because she didn't want to scare her friend, but she'd worried about the same thing. She was starting to think it would be smart for them to get the paperwork signed and done before they worried about the cat business, just in case.

"Are you sure you don't want me or Noah to drive?" Lou asked, placing a calm hand on Willow's arm. "That way you can relax."

Willow shook her head emphatically. "No, driving is the only way I won't go crazy." She shook the tension from her shoulders, relaxing into the driver's seat. "I'm okay. I promise."

Lou trusted her, and they hit the road. When they arrived at Milton Farm, Peggy Lee didn't have any seeds to spit or vegetables to throw. She wasn't smiling, though, which made Lou worry a bit. The older woman clutched the doorframe as she watched them ascend the stairs, as if she was worried they were here to take her house from her.

But once she locked eyes on Lou, her worry seemed to clear—not completely, but it was like clouds parting on an overcast day to show enough of the sun that you still believed it was there. Immediately, Lou changed the plan. Cat first, then paperwork.

"Peggy Lee, this is Holden Clawfield. You're welcome to change his name." Lou waited for her reaction.

A smile crept over her features. "Oh, Holden's quite a nice name. I think Benji would've liked it. He liked *The Catcher in the Rye*."

Noah opened the crate door, letting Holden out into the house. Normally, Noah advocated for letting cats have a smaller space to get used to before introducing them to the entire house, but Lou suspected that he—as much as she—wanted to see how Holden did, to gauge if this were even an option.

Would he like it? Would he and Peggy Lee even get along?

Already, the large farmhouse windows seemed to make him happier than the somewhat dark interior of the bookshop. Lou loved the big front windows of her shop, but she supposed it could be a little dark in some spots, especially if you were an outdoor-loving cat.

But it was when Peggy Lee walked over and plucked the cat off the floor that Lou really held her breath. Her gaze flicked over to Noah. He nodded once, slowly, as if telling her to give them a minute. Lou did.

Peggy Lee turned the cat one way and then the other, inspecting him. To Lou's surprise, he didn't struggle or squirm. In fact, she could hear him purring from across the room.

"Well, you do seem pretty." Peggy Lee pressed her lips forward in deliberation. "It remains to be seen how smart you are, though. Do you think you can stay close to me, so I can keep you safe?"

Holden let out a sweet meow as if in answer to her question.

Lou's heart melted, and from the way Peggy Lee tucked him under one arm after that, it seemed like hers had as well. Noah directed them to the table so he could ask some questions about cat ownership, have Peggy Lee sign the adoption paperwork, and give her some pointers about the differences between owning a cat versus a dog. He also went over things she needed to watch out for with a cat who was going to spend time outside.

"Okay, now for the less-fun part," Willow said, taking out her paperwork as Noah packed away his.

But Lou's and Willow's fears seemed unwarranted. Holden fell asleep on Peggy Lee's lap, making her smile. The expression didn't leave her face as she looked through Willow's plans, agreeing with almost everything Willow presented.

There were a few instances of "You want to grow that? Okay, it's your funeral." But besides those outbursts, Peggy Lee seemed happy enough with Willow's plan.

"Great," Peggy Lee said. "I'll get a rental agreement drawn up and contact you when I have the paperwork." She stood, setting the sleeping cat in the empty chair before reaching forward to shake Willow's hand.

Willow was in such a happy trance that Lou offered to drive on the way home, and Willow agreed.

Lou's fingers tightened around the steering wheel as she drove. "Anyone hungry?" she tried to ask in her most nonchalant tone.

Willow nodded. "I could eat."

"Me too," Noah said.

Lou bit back a smile. She knew just the place. Sure, she was craving a grilled-cheese sandwich, but she was even hungrier for information.

"I could text Easton." Willow pulled out her phone. "See if he can meet us somewhere. What do we feel like? Thai? We're close to Brine over here. We could grab some deep-fried pickles." She chuckled.

Lou panicked slightly. If Easton came, he might want to go somewhere closer to the police station, which meant Thai food. And while Lou loved their local Thai place, she needed to talk to Devon Goddard.

"I saw this cool food truck called Grown Up Grilled Cheese. I think he parks it up here by the gas station. He serves gourmet grilled-cheese sandwiches." Lou glanced over at Willow and then at Noah in the rearview mirror.

"Right. I heard about him," Noah said. "Marigold wanted to go, but I didn't think she'd like jalapeño or artichokes on her sandwich."

Lou looked at Willow, who was still studying her phone.

Willow must've felt her friend's gaze because she checked her phone again and said, "Easton will meet us there." She smiled up from her phone.

A wave of relief swept over Lou. He'd agreed to come to the food truck. But a fresh worry encompassed Lou as she realized she wasn't out of the woods yet. If Easton came, she wouldn't be able to question Devon, the owner of the truck, without him knowing she wasn't staying out of the case like she'd said she would.

Glancing quickly at Noah and Willow, Lou realized she was already walking that line of deception. Willow and Noah might not be in law enforcement, but they would probably be wary to see her getting involved in Nina's case again after what had happened in the corn maze.

The reminder made Lou question whether she should even pursue this clue. But as they pulled up to the gas station parking lot, where the food truck was parked, and Lou caught how crowded it was, she felt a lot better. Devon wouldn't do anything in front of all these people.

Parking, Lou and her friends stood near the menu written out on the side of the truck, deciding on their orders.

"Noah, they have a classic grilled cheese for Marigold," Lou said, pointing to the last item on the list.

"That's good to know," he said. "I'll definitely bring her back here."

There were a few picnic tables set up in the grassy area next to the parking lot. Devon announced each order with a honk of the truck's horn, which was one of those fun *awooga* sounds, before he called the person's name.

"I think I have to try the one with steak, Gorgonzola, and a blackberry balsamic reduction," Willow said, her eyes wide as she read through the list of ingredients.

"And I don't think I can say no to the Manchego-and-Gruyère sandwich with spicy sausage, caramelized onions, and a sunny-side-up egg," Noah said.

"Those both sound great. I'm still deciding on mine. Why don't you two grab a spot at one of the picnic tables? I'll go place our order," Lou offered.

"Thanks," Willow said. "Would you get the one with bacon and bleu cheese for Easton?"

She and Noah fished cash from their wallets to hand over to Lou. She took their money and got in line. By the time she got to the front, she'd decided on a sandwich with Gouda, Swiss, turkey, peppers, onions, and avocado. She rattled off the order the moment it was her turn, afraid she might forget someone's sandwich.

"What's the name?" Devon asked, pen poised above his ordering notebook.

Lou's skin flushed hot and cold. If Devon really was the killer, she didn't want him to have her name.

"Genevieve," she blurted out, always having liked that name.

Devon typed the order into his tablet. "Okay, will that be cash or card, Genevieve?" he asked.

The heat drained from Lou's face. Her actual name would be on her card. And then she would really attract his suspicion.

She had the cash from her friends, but it wouldn't be enough with the addition of her sandwich. Lou looked through the pockets in her wallet, trying not to appear frantic, as she searched for some cash. She was about to make up a story about not having her card with her, and having to go borrow money from her friend, when she found a few fives folded in a side pocket.

Thank goodness. She handed over the cash to pay. As he got her change, Lou looked over her shoulder. Once she confirmed there wasn't anyone else in line after her, she said, "I'm so glad I could try your food. I've heard such good things about it."

Devon handed her the change. "Thank you." He patted the wall. "It's my baby."

That phrase caught Lou's attention. "Yeah?" she asked. "Has it always been your dream to own a food truck?"

Devon tipped his head from side to side. "Well, I definitely thought I'd have my own restaurant someday. I pictured something a little more brick and mortar." He chuckled. "But this is better, in my mind. I can move with the crowds and do events easily."

"You seem to have put a lot into this," Lou observed.

"You're not kidding. Everything I have is right here. Well, except the place I rent. But other than that, I sold my car, cashed in my savings. It's all in this venture for me. I'm one hundred percent in."

"You sold your car?" Lou's chin jutted back.

He laughed. "Technically, this is still a vehicle, so I drive this if I really have to go anywhere. It's just temporary until I can get my feet under me a little more." He glanced up as a customer came up behind her. "Thanks for your order. I'll call your name as soon as it's ready."

Lou stepped aside so the next person could order. But as soon as she walked back to wait with her friends, the fake smile she'd been wearing fell away. Devon had just admitted to putting everything he had into this food truck. So if Nina had really threatened to bring it down, that might be something a man would fight to keep silent. If he killed her, the lawsuit she'd filed against him wouldn't go anywhere, and he might've succeeded in silencing her.

Easton had arrived, and he sat at the picnic table with Willow and Noah. She thought about telling him about this development in Nina's case. But when she sat down, her friends were making plans to carve the pumpkins they'd bought together on their outing to the corn maze, and Lou hated to ruin the fun time. Easton also looked exhausted, and this was obviously the only free time he'd had since the outing to the pumpkin patch and maze. She didn't want to ruin it with something that wasn't even his case.

Together, they decided on Tuesday evening for their pumpkin-carving party, giving Lou a few days to come up with a design idea. At that moment, she had nothing. The awooga horn pulled her back to reality.

"Genevieve," Devon called through the truck's window. "Order for Genevieve."

Lou's eyes widened. "Uh, I think that was the lady right in front of me. I'm going to wait up there, so he doesn't have to call me next." She walked over to get their food.

And while she seemed to fool Willow and Easton, who were planning a joint pumpkin design, Noah's eyes narrowed ever so slightly as he watched Lou get up from the table and leave.

CHAPTER 18

T he next day in the bookshop was lovely, and it felt like things were back to normal. The Japanese maple trees Willow had given Lou only got more vibrant each day, and they perfectly framed the view out the front windows of the bookshop. Their coloring made everything seem cozier, even if the day was a little overcast and gray.

Feline-wise, Lou settled back into her normal routine. As much as she'd loved having Holden Clawfield around, it had been clear that this wasn't the place for him. Peggy Lee had already sent multiple pictures to Lou, showing her how quickly the little guy was settling in.

So, it wasn't as if Lou needed much of a break after closing the shop that day, but she was still excited for her evening plans. She and Willow were scheduled to pick up the tiny house from Omer that evening.

Willow picked Lou up in the truck she'd bought for hauling her horse trailer, excitement radiating from her taut posture. Lou was a little nervous about the transporting issue, but Willow regularly towed a massive horse trailer around the county during their summer show circuit. She wasn't afraid of moving a tiny house across town.

"Oh, I forgot to ask, did you ever look into who called your cell a few months ago?" Willow glanced over at Lou as she drove through downtown Button.

Lou couldn't believe she'd forgotten to tell Willow. It must've slipped her mind with all the Milton Farm excitement yesterday. "Yes, it was Jonah Frazier, Nina's backyard neighbor."

Willow sucked in an excited breath.

"But he can't be the texter or the killer," Lou added quickly, not wanting to get Willow's hopes up. "Noah said he's been in prison for at least three months now."

"Oh, the jewelry store." Willow nodded as the name seemed to click in her memory. She slowed her truck as she pulled up to the Whelan's house.

Omer met them in the driveway. It hadn't rained for a couple of days, so the wet pavement and the fact that the tiny house shone like it was brand new told Lou that Omer must've pressure-washed the exterior to get it ready for Willow's arrival. He wore a huge grin that surprised Lou. He'd been so heartbroken to let this symbol of his freedom go that Lou had been dreading having to watch him give it up.

"Your payment came through just now," he said, holding his arms out wide as if he might hug Willow. Thinking better of it, he dropped them by his side. "You really didn't have to do that."

Willow swatted the air. "Do what? I was just paying for your labor."

Lou caught that her friend had paid the kid much more than what he'd listed on his blog for material costs. Willow was a good person. Money hadn't always come easy to Willow, especially when she had to buy her ex-fiancé out of the house they'd bought together when she learned he was cheating on her. But she'd finally paid off her parents for the loan they'd given her, and it looked like she was putting everything she could into this nursery endeavor. Plus, she had a meeting that week with the local bank, which would hopefully supply her with a business loan to help with start-up costs.

"It's going okay inside?" Lou asked, nodding toward his sister's house.

To her surprise, yet again, Omer broke into a smile. "Yeah, I'm enjoying it a lot more than I thought I would. I made a deal with them that I need set hours for my design work in the evening, but I help with babysitting the kids during the day. I'm having fun with my niece and nephew. To be honest, I think I was becoming a little hermit-like in there." He rounded his shoulders and mimed typing on a keyboard.

Willow laughed. "I'm glad I'm just using it for an office, then. I'll have to watch out for that."

Together, they helped direct Willow to back up and line up the truck hitch with the tiny house trailer.

"I'm glad things are working out for you," Lou said once the hitch was lined up and Willow jumped out to make the connection.

Omer relaxed next to Lou, seeing Willow knew what she was doing from here. "With the extra money Willow gave me, I'm going to do things right this time. I'll save up for property. Then I can build something that's not on wheels."

"Property? That'll be nice."

"Yeah, I like the tiny-house life, but I want to live in the woods, not around these houses. I would get woken up all the time in the middle of the night from people driving by in loud cars. Even with the insulation. One night, I even swore I heard one of those awooga horns."

Lou perked up, remembering the very distinct sound at the grilled-cheese food truck the night before. "What night was that? If you remember?"

Omer squinted an eye and said, "Uh, like a week ago? Yeah, I think it was last Sunday night. Well, Monday morning. I remember because I'd stayed up close to two, working on a design job and had only just gotten to sleep when I was woken up again."

"Omer, can you check if I connected the brake lights correctly?" Willow called as she went back to the truck and pressed down on the brake, then hit each turn signal. Omer gave her a thumbs-up for each action.

But Lou's mind felt stuck as it worked through the information Omer had just spilled. At first, she thought Devon wouldn't be silly enough to drive his very recognizable food truck to kill Nina, but then she remembered it was his only form of transportation. If he didn't drive that, he had nothing. Maybe he would've risked it, especially if it was the middle of the night, and he thought no one would notice.

This didn't match with the mystery texter, and how they'd told her they thought it was one of Nina's neighbors who'd killed her. But she doubted the motivation and trustworthiness of the mystery texter more by the day. It wasn't as if she'd contacted them in a couple of days, but they also hadn't contacted her either. Maybe they knew they'd gotten too close in the corn maze.

Behind her, Willow and Omer approached, shaking hands.

"Thank you so much," Willow said.

"Thank you," Omer agreed.

Lou shook his hand too. "Omer, before we go, I have one more question for you. You said we wouldn't believe what you'd heard Nina get in fights with people about, during the summer. Do you mind telling me what that was about?"

Omer's eyes widened. "Oh, sure." He took a step closer, as if he didn't want the neighborhood to hear. "Her neighbor, Chase, has to sell his house because she buried him in legal fees over a fence he had to take down and rebuild."

"Oh, that's it?" Lou asked, then added. "Nothing else?"

Omer lifted a brow at her like she was crazy, but then his focus moved to something behind them.

"Need a police escort?" a familiar voice called out.

Lou and Willow turned to see Easton. His cruiser window rolled down as he pulled to a stop in front of the driveway. Easton got out and kissed Willow hello. Omer, seemingly uncomfortable with their display of affection, headed inside.

"I think we're okay," Willow told Easton. "What are you doing around here?"

His eyes flicked across the street. "Just checking out a few leads. Can I stop by and see it once I'm done, though?"

Willow nodded, and they all parted ways. Lou couldn't help but notice that Easton drove over to the Frazier house, pulling in behind a red car in the driveway. She knew he was working on a completely different case but couldn't help but find it interesting that she'd also come across the Fraziers in her investigation about Nina.

All thoughts of cases and neighbors were put on hold as Lou and Willow spent the next hour figuring out where best to park the tiny house on the nursery property. It was hard to picture since it was the only piece so far, but Willow had a vision.

"I think once I have everything else in place, I'll take it off this trailer so it looks like a little cottage in the middle of the nursery," she said, rubbing her hands excitedly.

Easton pulled up just as they were leveling the trailer.

"What were you talking to the Fraziers about?" Lou asked him as conversationally as she could.

"Why?" Easton asked.

Lou scratched at her nose for a moment.

She hesitated long enough that Willow spoke for her. "Lou was trying to figure out how the mystery texter could've gotten her personal number. She used to put it up when she was trying out closing early on Mondays and Tuesdays. Jonah Frazier was one of the two people who called it, the other being Noah."

Lou was grateful that Willow had stepped in. It sounded less silly coming from her. But she was about to throw that all out the window with what she said next. "I know he's in prison, so he couldn't have physically been the one to strangle Nina, but I feel like it's a thing where criminals hire people in prison to kill people who put them there."

"Nina had nothing to do with Jonah's incarceration. I promise," Easton said. "I was checking into Judge Potts' last few cases and cross-referencing with registered firearms, since we still don't have the murder weapon. The Fraziers were a dead end. They reported the thing stolen three years ago. I just had to check."

Willow rubbed Easton's back. "Sorry. This case seems stressful."

Easton sighed. "We have no murder weapon. They committed the murder at three in the morning, which means no one really has a good alibi. Even people who are married could sneak out of bed without their spouse noticing. Nothing's foolproof."

"I thought you were investigating Judge Potts' wife, Becky?" Lou asked. "Didn't she have a questionable alibi?"

Willow's eyes widened. "Oh, he didn't tell you?"

"Becky Potts' alibi *was* a lie," Easton said.

Lou's breath caught in her throat. But any anticipation fell flat as she realized Easton still didn't have a clue who'd killed Judge Potts, so there must be another catch.

"Becky Potts was having an affair," Easton explained. "She lied because she didn't want anyone to know she was with Eric Randell, the man she was seeing that night. They were together all night in a hotel in Brine. There's security footage. But even though Becky's husband had found out about the affair because she got fired, Eric hadn't told his wife yet. They wanted time to do that." Easton shrugged. "It's still not airtight; few alibis are. But it's enough that I need to look in other places too."

Lou felt sorry for Easton. She felt similarly frustrated with Nina's case, even though she was, strictly speaking, not really supposed to be thinking about it.

She had an odd feeling that these two murders were connected, but she couldn't prove anything about Nina's case, and Easton wasn't getting anywhere with his. Maybe the only connection between the cases was that they were both at dead ends.

CHAPTER 19

When Lou got home a short while later, she was having a hard time not thinking about Nina's case.

It was like a puzzle that was sitting undone on the table, right in front of her. And even though she knew she shouldn't do any more physical investigating, she could write down what she knew, and see if there were any pieces that fit together once she looked at it all. So, she climbed the stairs to her apartment with her small herd of cats, and she did just that.

"Okay, so I know Nina died around three in the morning last Monday," she narrated as she wrote. The cats crowded around her as if they understood and were helping. Well, all except Sapphire, who'd already curled up next to Lou and was fast asleep.

"She was strangled with a thin, blue leash." Lou pictured Mr. Muffin's blue collar. "Most likely the leash she used for Mr. Muffins. But it's missing."

Anne Mice blinked at her, and her head dipped into what looked like a nod.

"Chase, Omer, and Devon all had a motive to kill her. And even though Detective Anderson thought a smaller person would be more likely to use a leash to strangle someone than a big person, who would just use their hands, it's not out of the question that a bigger person killed her," she explained to the cats. "I don't think the medical examiner would be able to tell that from the marks on her throat."

Catnip Everdeen jumped into the window as if Lou's case was boring her. Lou chuckled.

"Don't give up yet, Catnip," she teased. "Chase lives alone, so he could've gotten up in the middle of the night and strangled Nina over the fence debacle. Omer could've easily slipped out of the tiny house and gone across the street. Or, if what Omer heard that morning is true, Devon might've tried to silence her to get rid of her food poisoning lawsuit. He was in the neighborhood with his food truck around the time of death, unless there's someone else who has an awooga horn."

Anne Mice meowed, thinking Lou was talking to her.

"I agree," Lou said. "We need to know more about Devon. If he was on Pattern Drive at the time Nina was killed, that's too much of a coincidence for me. But the weirdest thing is that I could've sworn in the corn maze there was a man and a woman. The man had been whispering Nina's name, but it had been a woman who'd told him to grab me. And that was a man's arm that reached through the corn stalks. I'm just not sure how it all fits together."

She was tapping the pen against her bottom lip when she got a call.

"Hello."

"Lou?" The voice on the other end was small and sad, like it was hiding in a dark hole. Even in its smaller state, Lou recognized the gruffness behind it.

"Peggy Lee? Is everything okay?" Worries raced through Lou's mind about Holden. Had the cat run away? Was he hurt?

Peggy Lee sniffed. "I'm having a hard day. I was going through Benji's old planting diagrams, and I found a note he wrote to me. He used to leave these cute notes on the fridge, saying things like, 'Little Darling, I'm out in the field. See you soon.' It sent me into a spiral. Holden helped at first, but then I started looking through old photos, and it got worse. Do you think you could come have dinner with me?"

Lou breathed out a sigh of relief. It wasn't as if she was happy that Peggy Lee was hurting, but she could definitely help with emotional pain. At least there wasn't an emergency or something wrong with her cat. Lou's stomach grumbled at the mention of food. She'd let herself become preoccupied with Nina's case once she got home from helping Willow with the tiny house, and she hadn't even thought of dinner.

"Absolutely. I'll leave now. What can I bring?" Lou made sure the cats had full bowls of food as she grabbed her purse.

"Oh, anything sounds fine. I'm not picky." Just the promise of Lou coming over seemed to ease the tension in Peggy Lee's tone. Her voice sounded more normal.

Lou flicked through the options. She could pick up something on the way. Devon's food truck had been a hit, and Peggy Lee might really like some grown-up grilled cheese. She could also talk to him a little more about why he was in the neighborhood the night Nina was killed. She explained the concept to Peggy Lee, who said she'd love whichever sandwich Lou got.

"Okay, I'm on my way," Lou said, grabbing more cash as she hung up the call.

As she drove, she thought through what she might say to Devon to get the truth out of him about Nina. She had a lingering worry that it wasn't very smart to corner a potential murderer with questions that placed him at the scene of the crime. But when she pulled into the lot where the truck was parked, it was hopping just like the other evening when Willow, Noah, and Lou had met Easton there.

Lou let a couple go in front of her in line, hoping to recreate the situation she had last time, where Devon might have a moment to talk to her.

"Genevieve, right?" Devon asked when she stepped up to order.

Lou smiled, grateful he'd reminded her of her pseudonym.

"Back for more?" he asked.

"I am. I have another friend who needs to try your food." She recited her order. "I'm adding to your fan club."

"I appreciate it." He took her money and started on her order.

Lou chewed on her lip, trying to figure out a segue into the fact that Omer had heard his truck in the neighborhood the night Nina was killed. Devon held up a finger and reached over to honk the horn and called out a name for another order.

"That's a pretty unique horn," she said, latching on to the opportunity.

Devon chuckled. "Came with the truck, but it's been fun for calling out orders. I don't have the loudest voice."

"Is it a pretty common horn sound? I've never heard it before," Lou said.

"Not common at all. I've mostly seen people put them into classic cars. I think mine is the only one in Button," he said proudly.

Lou bit back a triumphant grin. She had him. "So then, you must've been out by Pattern Drive a week ago, in the middle of the night?" When she could see she had Devon's attention, she said, "Someone said that sound woke them out of a deep sleep the other day."

Devon blinked, stopping what he was doing with the grill. Lou worried for a second that he might burn her order if he didn't pay closer attention. "What do you mean?"

"A friend of mine lives in a tiny house, and he heard that sound in the middle of the night last Sunday night, early Monday morning. The walls of his tiny house aren't as thick or insulated as a regular house. If you're the only one in town with a horn like that, it had to be you, right?"

Devon's cheeks, already pink from the warm grill, turned positively red with embarrassment.

Seeing that Devon was clamming up, Lou kept going. "And you said this is your only vehicle, so you'd be forced to take it anywhere you wanted to go." She folded her arms over her chest. "You also knew Nina Upton, who lived on that road, didn't you? Look, I know about her lawsuit against you."

Devon's shoulders slumped forward in defeat. "I'll admit it. I drove by her house. I was going to leave a threatening note telling her to drop the case." He scanned the area behind Lou like he was worried someone would overhear. "I didn't even end up leaving the note."

"Why?" Lou leaned forward. The answer might be because he'd killed her and hadn't needed to go again, but Lou didn't want to put those words in his mouth.

He ran the back of his gloved hand across his forehead, then looked down and tossed the gloves in the trash. "I got scared, okay?" The same embarrassment flushed across his cheeks. "There was someone crawling out of the storm drain. I just finished reading *It* by Stephen King, and I freaked out. That's why the horn sounded. I was halfway out the door before I saw the person climbing out, and I booked it out of there."

Lou digested the information as Devon wrapped up her order. "You saw someone in the storm drain? Did you get a good look at who it was?" she asked, wondering why he hadn't gone to the police about this. Then again, Nina's time of death was something she only knew because of how close she was to the case.

Devon handed over her sandwiches and said, "I couldn't see anything more than the back half of a figure crawling out of the drain, backwards." Devon shivered. "I didn't stick around to see what the upper half looked like. It was just a shadow from where I was parked."

A frown crossed Lou's face as confusion settled over her. There had been a storm drain next to the pile of leaves where she'd found Nina's body. According to Omer, Devon had honked his horn right inside the window of Nina's time of death. Which meant, Devon might not have seen a murderous clown coming out of the storm drain, but he might've seen a killer. That made Lou suddenly very interested in the storm drain and whatever the shadowy figure had been doing inside it.

"Look, I really don't want any trouble," Devon said, seeing she wasn't leaving. "I know it was wrong to attempt to convince Nina to drop the case, but I really don't think it was my food that got her sick, and something like that could've been enough to ruin me. I've spent enough time feeling terrible that I was relieved to hear she was dead. I promise, I had nothing to do with it."

Lou couldn't do much more than nod and step aside, seeing there were other customers behind her now. She walked back to her car in a bit of a daze. She was still in a weird headspace when she pulled up to Milton Farm.

Peggy Lee sat on the porch swing. Holden Clawfield was with her, lounging in her lap, kneading and purring away.

Lou smiled as she took in the scene. "He seems to be settling in nicely."

Peggy Lee nodded, but there was no happiness behind her eyes, reminding Lou why she was there. A bad day. Lou had definitely had her fair share of those. She sat in the rocking chair next to the swing, handing Peggy Lee her sandwich.

"Why were you looking through Benji's old planting diagrams?" Lou kept her sandwich in her lap, wanting to give Peggy Lee her full attention.

Peggy Lee must've needed the food, because she took a bite, chewed, and swallowed before saying, "Willow's reminded me a lot of his."

Lou tipped her head to the side. "I'm so sorry, Peggy Lee. If Willow knew this would bring up such hard feelings for you, she wouldn't want to move forward. Do you want me to call her?"

Peggy Lee held up a hand. "No, it's good. Just hard."

Lou knew exactly what the woman meant by that.

"Tell me more about these notes he used to write to you," Lou said, unwrapping her sandwich and taking her first bite. Lou was worried talking about memories might throw Peggy Lee back into a sadness spiral, but it also had the potential to be the bright light she could take to find her way out of the darkness.

"He always called me that, Little Darling." Peggy Lee's cheeks heated. "I know I'm not the typical idea of feminine, but Benji always made me feel beautiful."

Lou reached forward and placed a hand on Peggy Lee's. "He sounds like he was a very special person. But that doesn't mean he's the only one who is ever going to see the good in you either."

Peggy Lee's gaze dropped to her lap, and Lou removed her hand. "I don't think I'm interested in falling in love again."

"That's not what I meant," Lou clarified. "You may have had the love of your life, but you can still have friends who make you feel as important as Benji did."

"I see. You're right." Peggy Lee met Lou's eyes. "What about you? Do you think you'll ever fall in love again? You're a lot younger than me." She let out a rough laugh.

Lou gave a half smile. "Honestly, I don't know. I'm not closing myself off to it, but it seems hard when you've already found the person you loved more than you could ever imagine. I don't know if I believe that there's another person just as perfect for me out there."

They finished their sandwiches, talking about their favorite memories of their husbands.

"Okay. You're right, talking about it is much better than keeping it inside." Peggy Lee balled the sandwich wrapper into her palm. "And thank you for dinner. That was fantastic. It's a food truck down the road, you said?"

"Parked at the gas station," Lou said absentmindedly. She couldn't seem to get her thoughts straight about what Devon had told her.

Peggy Lee cleared her throat. When Lou looked up, she'd placed a hand on her hip and was cocking an eyebrow at Lou.

"Now you're the one keeping something inside," Peggy Lee said with a small smirk. "Spill it."

Lou sighed and said, "It's this murder case I got dragged into."

"The one with the judge?" Peggy Lee asked.

"No, Nina Upton's death. Did you hear about that one?" Lou scratched at Holden's ears, and he purred softly.

"Nina's dead?" Peggy Lee puffed out her cheeks. "She used

to be our CPA, well, for a couple of months. But Benji didn't like her, and so the firm switched us to Becky Potts." Peggy Lee shrugged. "Odd how things are connected like that."

Lou needed a moment to catch up. "Wait. What did you just say? Becky and Nina worked together?"

"Yes. Becky Potts was our CPA for decades."

"Was?"

Peggy Lee raised her palms. "I just got a letter from the firm saying she was leaving."

"Because of her husband's murder?" Lou's heartbeat increased, making it hard for her to hear.

"No," Peggy Lee said. "I got this letter a couple of weeks ago. And it came with some kind of reminder of their company code of ethics. I was wondering if she stole money, but that wouldn't be like Becky at all."

Lou's mind whirred as she thought about the affair Easton had mentioned yesterday. He'd said Becky's husband knew about the affair because she'd been fired because of it. Sleeping with a client certainly seemed like it would break a company's ethical code. But what if it had been one of her coworkers who'd told on her? That certainly would be a reason Becky might want Nina out of the picture.

"Sorry, I got off topic." Peggy Lee waved a hand toward Lou. "So someone killed Nina, and you're wrapped up in it?"

Lou explained how she was a suspect because of the fight she'd had with Nina the day before, and how she'd gotten the mystery texts, telling her to look into Nina's neighbors. She pulled out the hand-drawn map Noah had made for her as she explained the people she thought could've killed Nina, adding in Devon, even though he didn't live in the neighborhood.

"Have you talked to Beau?" Peggy Lee pointed to the Frazier house.

"Who?" Lou asked.

"Beau Frazier. Last I heard, he was living with his uncle, Lester." Peggy Lee sat back. "He worked here with Benji after he got out of going to prison by doing some community service. Judge Potts knew Benji was good at working with people who need second chances. That boy was quiet, but very observant. He might've noticed something that could help you."

Lou leaned forward. "I had no idea about Beau. Everyone who's talked about the Fraziers always mentions Lester and Jonah. I know Jonah's in prison for robbing a jewelry store. I didn't even know he had a cousin."

Peggy Lee clicked her tongue. "People tend not to talk much about Beau. Truth is, I think the lot of them fear the boy. He's huge. He has these hands that could crush a skull, and he got into one massive fight in high school. That's what set him in front of Judge Potts. But that boy had the gentlest way with plants. He wasn't a violent person at heart. He grew up in an unpleasant situation, and I think he has some trauma to get over, but after that fight, people saw him as a monster."

"But you didn't see that side of him?" Lou asked.

"Not one bit." Peggy Lee cut the air with her hand. "He had these sad, gray eyes that made you feel you were looking right into that boy's soul. He might be big, but he always reminded me of Ferdinand, the bull that just wants to sit and smell flowers." Her expression darkened. "People around him were the ugly ones, always calling him crazy."

Forrest's words about a person who'd been made to feel crazy came back to her.

Lou had a gut feeling that Beau Frazier had to be her mystery texter. And as much as she'd been sure that the texter was also the murderer, she hoped that wasn't the case anymore.

Because she'd just learned something that made the woman and the man in the corn maze, make a lot more sense.

What if Judge Potts' murder and Nina's murder were connected like Lou originally thought? And what if Becky Potts and Eric Randell had been the couple in the corn maze who'd come after her?

CHAPTER 20

Lou couldn't let go of her theory about Becky Potts and Eric Randell working together to kill Craig Potts and Nina Upton. The only snag was that Becky and Eric had been in that hotel for the night, which meant they also had an alibi for the time Nina was killed. Lou couldn't help but wonder if there was a way to fake security footage. There was in the movies. Could Becky have snuck out to kill Nina while Eric took out Becky's husband?

She was glad the bookshop was open for at least a few hours that Monday morning so she could run all these theories by her regulars. She started with Becky Potts.

"I don't want to repeat gossip if it's not true, but did anyone else hear that Judge Potts' wife, Becky, was fired from her job at the accounting firm?" Lou asked nonchalantly after her regulars came in and settled down, but before any other customers showed up.

George, Silas, and Forrest looked up at Lou.

"Yeah. That's not gossip, Lou. Everyone knows that." George blinked, smiling like Lou's concern was unwarranted.

"George is right." Forrest bobbed his head.

"Yeah," Silas said. "Gossip would be to say that she got fired for sleeping with one of her clients and that everyone believes she and the guy offed her husband because he was threatening to leave her with nothing in the divorce."

Forrest pinched the bridge of his nose.

Lou didn't want to add to the rumors, but she thought maybe it went even deeper than that. If the two cases were linked, she needed to talk to Easton as soon as possible. She picked up her phone to text him, only to see another text message waiting for her. The words on her screen made her blood run cold.

> I think we should meet. I'm ready to tell you
> who I think it is. The lake off Bias Road. 10
> tonight. Come alone.

Mark my words. In the next couple of days, they'll ask you to meet. That will be your clue that they're the murderer, Easton had said.

Lou glanced up from her phone. "What do you guys know about Beau Frazier?"

George cringed. Silas tsked. Forrest adopted a sad expression. The regulars let the latter speak.

"Beau Frazier is a troubled young man, but I believe he has a good heart," Forrest said. "I never saw him professionally," he added, holding up a hand so Lou wouldn't think he was breaking patient confidentiality. "That's just my observation from afar."

"I don't know much about Beau. He didn't come to live with Lester and Jonah until we were in high school," George supplied. "But I knew Jonah, and I'd say the same thing about him. He's a good guy who gets himself in the wrong situations."

Silas snorted. "Yeah, but Jonah's the size of a regular person, not a Frankenstein monster. And he just drove a getaway car. He didn't pummel some poor kid."

Lou flinched at the image Silas's blunt words conjured.

"That's not fair," George said. "Beau was just trying to protect his cousin. The guy he hit was getting Jonah into some illegal stuff. Also, he didn't pummel him. I think he got in a handful of punches at most. The other kid's parents were just really into pressing charges and making Beau out to be a monster," George added.

Silas slipped his hands into his pockets. "He said he didn't remember hitting him more than once, and he definitely did."

"If Beau has a history of trauma, as I'm sure he does, given the small amount I know of his past, it's possible he did black out a little during the violence." Forrest folded his hands in his lap.

George nodded. "And Judge Potts, who is well known for being super strict, gave him community service instead of jail time. It was a misunderstanding."

That tracked with what Peggy Lee had told Lou.

"So you think he's harmless?" Lou asked George, then turned her attention to Forrest. Not that she didn't want Silas's point of view on the matter, but he tended to be a little more judgmental about people and their actions.

George's gaze dropped to her sneakers. "I can't say harmless. I just think he's misunderstood."

Lou glanced over at her phone. Regardless of what her regulars thought, there was no way she was going to meet this mystery texter, even if it was Beau, and people she trusted seemed to think the town had the wrong idea about the guy.

Once Lou was off work that afternoon, she took a long run, happy that it was in the middle of the day. She stopped at the police station, jogging in place a few moments before pushing open the door and heading inside. The fact that she had questions about whether the two cases were linked made Lou sure Easton needed to know. It was a bonus she wouldn't have to talk to Detective Anderson if she could tell everything to Easton.

Officer Reynolds sneered as he noticed her walking toward his desk. Somehow, she was sure the ornery officer and Detective Anderson were friends. They certainly had enough in common with how poorly they treated people who were just trying to help.

Steeling her resolve, Lou stopped in front of the reception desk and pushed back her shoulders. "I need to speak with Detective West about his case."

Officer Reynolds cocked an eyebrow. "Why?"

Lou took a breath. "I think I may have learned something important."

"Why don't you just text him, then?" Reynolds narrowed his eyes. "We all know you've got his number."

Lou's stomach turned at the suggestion. When she'd first moved to Button, the rest of the police department had thought Easton was spending too much energy on Lou, dropping everything whenever she needed help. The reality behind it had been that he saw Lou as a fresh start for him and Willow, a way to show Willow that he wasn't just her antagonistic next-door neighbor. And by being nice and accommodating to Lou, Willow might look at him differently. Which, to his credit, had happened. But the close-minded Officer Reynolds and his cronies couldn't see past the surface facts that each time Lou called, Easton had dropped everything to help her.

But that wasn't what had her hesitating. Sure, she could text Easton, but she needed to talk it out. She wasn't sure what she had and what was important. For a moment, she felt sympathetic with her mystery texter. Between the gruff response from the police and not being sure about the information she had, she could see why they wouldn't want to go to the police. If it really was Beau texting her, there would be even more prejudice and judgment against him. Not only did he have a reputation for being unhinged, but he'd been in trouble with the law before. Lou knew excellent police officers like Easton wouldn't hold something like that against a person, but Detective Anderson and Officer Reynolds proved to her that not all of them were as understanding.

"I, uh, wanted to tell him in person," Lou answered flatly.

Reynolds scoffed. "Well, too bad. He's out of the office."

"Back again. Trying to bring Detective West in on your scheme?" a familiar voice said behind Lou.

She stiffened and turned to see Detective Roy Anderson walking up to the desk. He aimed his chin toward Officer Reynolds in a friendly greeting, confirming her suspicion about how well they would get along.

"Says she has some important information about his case," Reynolds answered for her. She didn't appreciate his mocking tone one bit.

"I do. And I think the two cases might be linked. So since you're here and he's not, I'm going to have to tell you," she said in her best *don't mess with me, I'm a New Yorker* tone.

Detective Roy Anderson held out his hand toward the hallway that she knew led to his and Easton's offices. She walked in front of him, using the time to line up the thoughts in her head. By the time she plopped down in the seat across from his desk, Lou was sure the detective was going to laugh her out of his office.

"I'm going to start by assuming you know that Nina Upton

and Becky Potts were coworkers at Button Accounting," Lou said.

Detective Anderson nodded.

"And they recently fired Becky Potts for having an affair with a client, the very man whom she was supposedly with on the night of the murder of both Nina Upton and Judge Craig Potts," Lou added.

"Supposedly?" Roy asked.

"She didn't come forward with that alibi at first. The reason she gave was that Eric's wife didn't yet know of the affair, and she wanted to give him time to break the news to his wife. But what if there was more to it? What if they didn't use that alibi at first because it wasn't the truth?"

The detective sighed. "Mrs. Henry, there's surveillance footage of them arriving at the hotel well before the murders."

"But is there a back window they could've snuck out of?" Lou asked. When she could see he was only becoming more exasperated by her, she said, "I believe that Nina Upton was the one who told on Becky, outing her affair to her bosses and her husband. Sticking her nose in other people's business and threatening people based on what she found out was what Nina did. What if Becky and Eric left the motel at some point during the night and split up? Becky went to kill Nina for what she'd done, and Eric went to kill Judge Potts so they would still have access to his money?"

Given the fact that Detective Anderson was looking at her like she was crazy already, Lou didn't think it wise to bring up the couple from the corn maze, or how she thought it could've been Becky Potts and Eric Randell trying to take her out of the equation.

"That's it?" Detective Anderson asked, folding his arms in front of himself. "That's the hard-hitting information you felt

Detective West couldn't live without?" He exhaled a puff of air in lieu of an actual laugh. "Did your mystery texter, who is definitely not you, tell you all of this?"

Lou clenched her teeth. "What about the storm drains near Nina's house? Did anyone from your crime scene team look through them?"

He didn't even humor her with an answer about that. "Look, we made sure there wasn't a back window in the room Becky and Eric were in. Easton watched the footage. They didn't leave." He tilted his head like he was talking to a toddler. "We know how to do our jobs. Please let us."

Lou felt utterly deflated by that news. No back window? And Easton had watched the footage. If Eric and Becky hadn't left, maybe she was wrong. If they had strong alibis, Lou's gut feelings and remaining theories were moot. Detective Anderson was right. She needed to let them handle this case. Who was she to think she could solve it?

"I'm sorry," she said. "I'll stay out of your way." And she left the police station, vowing to do just that.

CHAPTER 21

Lou may have made a mental promise to let the Nina case drop, but her mystery texter didn't get the memo because, the next morning, Lou awoke to a new text.

Maybe there was some incredulity left over from her meeting with Detective Anderson, or maybe it was just too early for her to care, but she needed some answers. She set her toothpaste down after putting some on her toothbrush and typed out,

The texter answered before Lou could even bring her toothbrush up to her mouth, showing they'd been typing at the same time she had.

I've been nothing but helpful to you. I'm trying to help you clear your name. Why would I tell you anything when you leave me waiting for an hour out in the cold? Why do you need to know?

The difference in the texter's attitude caused the hair on Lou's arms to stand on end. When she'd asked questions they didn't want to answer before, they'd just stayed silent. Even though they were still avoiding the answers, they seemed to be attacking her. The moment she confronted them for a name, they'd changed their tone completely? She rolled her eyes and gave them a piece of her mind.

First, you know who I am, so it only feels fair I know who you are. Second, I never said I would meet you, so it's on you if you waited. And third, why would I meet someone I don't know, in the dark?

Unlike the last message, there was a pause before the reply came through. Lou pondered the idea that the texter could also be the killer. Easton had been right, and with Detective Anderson shutting down her theory about Becky Potts and Eric Randell, this was the closest thing she had to a suspect.

Her phone buzzed with a reply, and Lou expected the texter to continue down the frustrated, angry road they'd started down. But she had to blink at the phone in order to make sure she was reading correctly.

You're right. I'm sorry. We could meet in the daylight if you're more comfortable with that. Same place? Or would you like somewhere more populated?

Lou reread the message. The mystery texter—Beau or otherwise—had changed their tone yet again. Their switch reminded her of Devon's change in tone on Sunday, and of what he'd said about the person hanging around the storm drain. She hadn't missed that Detective Anderson had failed to confirm or deny whether they'd checked the drains. Which meant she needed to look inside that storm drain. If Devon was telling the truth, why was a shadowy figure crawling out of the drain in the middle of the night?

She typed out a reply.

> Same place is fine if we can do this during the day. I can be there by one this afternoon. How will I find you?

Of course, Lou had no intention of meeting this person, not even in the light of day. But if it was Beau, and if he really had killed Nina, she needed to get him away from his house, and that storm drain, long enough to be able to check to see if there was anything there.

> I'll wear red to match my car.

Lou felt her breath catch in her throat. A red car. When Easton had pulled up to the Frazier's house the other day, there had been a red car parked in the driveway. It had to be Beau. She was sure of it. And even though she was luring the probable killer away from the house while she checked the storm drain, Lou wanted to bring backup, just in case.

She texted Willow, asking what her plans were that afternoon.

I've got that meeting with the bank about the
business loan. Wish me luck!

Willow responded, obviously assuming Lou just wanted to hang out after she closed the shop.

Lou could've kicked herself. Of course. She knew about the bank meeting. She'd gotten so distracted with this case that she'd forgotten a monumental day for her best friend.

You're going to do great!

I could do dinner, though. It sounds like
Easton's going to be working late. He's going
upstate for something.

Lou tapped her fingers on the desk. Now that she knew her theory about Becky and Eric was wrong, it became less likely that the two cases were linked. Lou hoped Easton going upstate meant he was getting close to a culprit in his case too.

Next, Lou texted Noah the same question as she had with Willow about plans that afternoon.

I have a client at noon, but it should be quick.
Then I'm free until around three. Why?

Lou grinned.

Mind accompanying me on a little scavenger
hunt?

I had a hunch you weren't going to let this case
drop.

Lou's cheeks heated as she remembered him watching her

the other day at Devon's food truck. But she smiled as he followed up that text with a second one.

> Anytime. Pick you up when I'm done?

> I'll meet you at your place around one, if that works.

He said it did, and Lou went about her day with the peace of mind that she'd have a friend with her to answer the final unanswered question lingering in her mind about Nina's death. Once she looked in that drain, she could let it all go.

She still had to get through the morning at the bookshop. On one hand, it would be good to get her mind off the meeting she wouldn't show up to. On the other, she didn't know how well she'd be able to concentrate on books and customers when this task was looming overhead. Worse, it was incredibly slow. Even her regulars didn't show.

The morning dragged by. She couldn't seem to focus. Everything reminded her of the case. She felt like someone was watching her, but each time she turned around, there wouldn't be anyone outside the shop or otherwise.

At lunchtime, she closed the shop and tried to eat, but found that she was too nervous to eat anything. Still, she couldn't leave too early and show up before Beau Frazier left the house for their meeting. He knew what she, and presumably her car, looked like.

Lou had just pulled into Noah's driveway when she got a text from him.

> I'm so sorry. We had a walk-in that needs emergency surgery. I'm going to be operating for the next couple of hours. Raincheck on the scavenger hunt?

No problem. Soon. Good luck with the surgery.

She exhaled her disappointment. But before starting up her car again, Lou couldn't help but scan the neighborhood. It was the middle of the day. Her mystery texter, presumably Beau Frazier, was at the meeting spot. If she was quick, she could just check the storm drain and go home.

Making a decision, she got out of her car and walked down the street toward Nina's house. The hairs on Lou's arms stood on end, and she rubbed her hands up and down the sleeves of her jacket to warm away the goose bumps.

The red car wasn't parked in front of the Frazier house, Lou didn't see a car out front, just like the day she'd found Nina's body. Glancing over her shoulder, Lou crouched next to the storm drain and peered inside. Nothing was visible through the metal grate.

Lou pulled out her phone and clicked on her flashlight. She shone the light down into the drain. She was feeling as if this must be a dead end, when the flashlight reflected off a small, silver clasp, like the kind that attached a leash to a dog collar.

Sure enough, as Lou peered closer, she could see a small section of blue leash, just like the one she had for Sapphire. She silently thanked Devon. Because of his fear of Stephen King characters, he'd led her right to the murder weapon.

CHAPTER 22

Although she hated to do so, Lou knew she had to call Detective Anderson. She didn't have his number, like she did with Easton, so she found the number to the Button Police Department.

"Reynolds speaking. If this is an emergency, please hang up and dial nine-one-one. If this is not an emergency, how may I help you?" The bored voice of Officer Reynolds didn't boost Lou's mood.

"May I please speak with Detective Anderson?" she asked, making her voice a little higher so he might not recognize her.

"Cat lady?" Reynolds asked through a cough. "You again?"

Lou rolled her eyes. "Yes, it's me. I need to speak with the detective, please. It's urgent."

"If it's—" he started.

But Lou cut him off. "It's not an emergency. I'm not hanging up to call nine-one-one. I just need to speak with Detective Anderson."

Officer Reynolds clicked his tongue. "Okay, yeesh. Stay

calm," he said before a few beeps preceded another ringing sound.

"Anderson," the detective answered the call. Lou wondered if the flat tone to his voice was how he always answered the phone or if Officer Reynolds had warned him it was her on the line.

"Detective Anderson, I think I've found the murder weapon you were looking for in connection with Nina Upton's murder. A blue dog leash? It appears to have been thrown down the storm drain near where I discovered her body." She grew self-conscious of the silence that stretched on after she finished speaking. "This is Louisa Henry, by the way."

"Yeah, I got that," Detective Anderson said dryly. "It's probably a shock to you, but I don't have many nosy women who insist they can do my job better than I can. I knew it was you right away."

"Okay." Lou blinked. "So are you coming to find the murder weapon, or am I going to crawl into this storm drain myself?" she said, mostly joking.

"Do nothing of the sort. Leave the premises, now." His tone grew cold. Then he hung up the call.

Lou glanced down at the drain. Unlike the ones in New York City, which connected to larger tunnels and the sewer system, this didn't seem to be big enough to hold a person. Devon would've been glad to know. This drain had a holding reservoir where debris sank to the bottom and mesh-covered pipes sat about halfway down on either side where the water could drain out to the nearest lake.

As she was studying the reservoir, Lou noticed another glint of metal. Could there be something else down there as well? Devon had mentioned the figure seemed to be crawling backwards out of the storm drain. What if they'd reached down to hide something under the debris? If the killer had been able to reach inside, she should be able to as well, right? Unless Beau Frazier really was huge, and his long arms meant he could reach farther.

Lou wouldn't be satisfied until she knew. Testing out the grate, she threaded her fingers through the metal holes and pulled with all her might.

The metal grate moved.

Lou's fingers shook from the effort, but she was able to lift it and move it slightly off-center so it hung over the lip of the street a couple of inches.

She extricated her fingers, pulsing them into fists to stop the ache that had built in her joints from the effort. Lou was about to try again, hoping to move the grate aside, when the sound of tires crunching on the pavement caught her ear. She didn't want to chance waiting until she could see the car, as that would mean the driver would be able to see her.

Jumping up, she raced into the hedge next to Nina's house. She peered out from behind the leaves as a red car careened forward, pulling to a stop in front of the Frazier house. Red, like the mystery texter's car. A man got out, but it was clear that it wasn't Beau Frazier. The man wasn't large like Lou had heard Beau was. In fact, this man, maybe ten years older than she was, seemed to be about her size. He wore a red zip-up sweatshirt.

A chill shivered down Lou's spine as she remembered Detective Anderson's analysis of the killer. *Smaller people, about your height, often use things to strangle people because their hands aren't big or powerful enough.*

Lester Frazier? Lou guessed, knowing Noah had mentioned that he was Jonah Frazier's father. Easton had also mentioned that Lester had been one of the people he'd checked with about guns since he was involved in a recent trial presided over by

Judge Potts. Right. His son's trial, where the young man was put away for twenty years.

That seemed like a motive to kill Judge Potts, but why had Lester killed Nina? Was she involved in putting away Jonah, like Lou had previously thought?

Lou shook her head. Just because he was coming back from someplace like he was the one who'd asked her to meet, didn't mean he was automatically the murderer.

Lester's car door slammed shut, making Lou jump. Lester's footsteps paused for a moment, and he turned back toward her. Her heartbeat pounded in her ears. She'd made a noise. He was coming to find her. She looked around, unsure if she should run or which direction to pick. His worn tennis shoes came into view through the dense leaves of the shrub.

He walked past.

Lou silently exhaled. But any relief she felt was washed away as Lester stopped next to the storm drain. Lou gritted her teeth as he knelt to inspect the grate. She'd left it askew. It was clear someone had tried to look inside.

Lester's body language was already angry, all quick movements and tensed muscles. But when he looked up and scanned the surrounding area, his red expression was downright livid. In that moment, she gave up hope that Lester might not be the killer. He knew what was in that drain and was spooked to see the cover had been moved. Could that second glint of metal she'd seen in the bottom of the storm drain be from the gun he'd used to kill Judge Potts?

Lester stood and searched the street, trying to locate whoever had been the one to move the grate. His sneakers struck the pavement as he ran down closer to Noah's house. Lou closed her eyes, hoping he wouldn't recognize her car.

A whispered "Pssst" made her jump, but she didn't scream.

Even her surprise instincts knew such a sound could be fatal. Turning around, she saw a hulking young man kneeling on the other side of the bushes where she was hiding. She wasn't sure if it was the gray eyes Peggy Lee had mentioned or his size, but she knew right away it was Beau Frazier.

He held out a hand toward her and jerked his head to the right, motioning for her to come with him.

A thousand scenarios ran through Lou's mind. Beau could be in on the crime with his uncle; he might be violent like all the kids in George's high school thought, or he was mentally unstable, like Silas had heard.

But in that moment, Lou listened to her gut—and Peggy Lee. She reached out and took his hand.

CHAPTER 23

Beau led Lou out of her hiding place in the bush. They raced around the small fence Nina had lining this side of her property, then dropped to their hands and knees once they were hidden behind its wooden planks.

Lou stiffened as Lester's footsteps pounded against the pavement and he ran back in their direction. Beau motioned for her to follow him as he crawled toward Nina's house. Lou stayed lower than he could because of his size, but as they edged through the grass, she felt exposed and uncomfortable.

A front door slammed somewhere to their right. Lester had gone inside his house. From Beau's quick movements, it seemed like he could tell his uncle wouldn't be inside for long. To Lou's surprise, Beau led her toward Nina's back door, pausing as he produced a key.

Quickly, for his size, he unlocked the door, swung it open, and stepped aside, gesturing for Lou to enter. In any different circumstance, she might've hesitated or thought through what she was doing. But in that moment, this seemed like her safest option. It didn't hurt that Lester had come out of his house—the door slamming shut once more—and they needed to hide.

Lou and Beau crouched in Nina's kitchen, peering out of the window above her sink that looked out on the street, almost level with the storm drain.

Lester looked over his shoulder a few more times before crouching by the grate and pulling the thing free. He knelt and reached down into the storm drain. He pulled out two items, a blue leash and a gun, putting them directly into the bag. He stood and looked over his shoulder before leaning down to put the grate back.

"He's getting away with the murder weapons," Lou whispered. She felt for her phone in her pocket. She dialed 9-1-1. After waiting for the dispatcher to ask their first question, Lou blurted out, "Send as many units as you can to the corner of Pattern Drive and Bobbin Road. The person who killed Judge Potts and Nina Upton is holding the murder weapons." Lou's eyes widened. "No, wait. He's putting them in the trunk of his car. He's going to get away. You need to get someone here now."

Lou knew it wasn't right, but she hung up and tried Easton. He didn't answer, but she sent him a text.

> Lester Frazier is the killer of both Judge Potts and Nina. He hid the gun and leash in the storm drain. Come to Nina's now!

Lou looked over at Beau. "Well, that's all we can do. Hopefully, the police will get here soon."

Beau nodded, and they both jumped in surprise as Lester slammed the trunk of his car.

Lou's phone buzzed in her hands, startling her a second time in as many seconds. Because of the surprise, she dropped her phone into Nina's stainless steel sink. It made the loudest noise Lou'd heard in a while. She cringed, trying to grab it. But when she looked up, Lester was staring straight at her through Nina's kitchen window.

The world seemed to go all wobbly with fear as he raced toward the back entrance. Lou glanced around, realizing Beau was gone. Had he abandoned her? Had he been part of this the whole time?

She flinched as the back window shattered, and Lester opened the door. Looking around her, Lou locked on to the biggest knife in the block. She wasn't sure what she planned to do with it, but she felt having some line of defense against Lester would be better than nothing. Grabbing the knife, she stood her ground in the kitchen, knowing it was too late to run or hide.

Lester wore a sick smile as he walked into the kitchen. "You found my hiding spot."

Lou swallowed, not wanting to give him any further reason to come after her. "I don't know what you mean."

"It's okay. I know you're the one who moved the grate," Lester said. "Smart. While I was off waiting to meet with you." He let out a humorless laugh. "Not smart enough, though." He stalked toward her, eyeing her knife.

He was reaching for a knife of his own when Beau jumped out of the hallway behind him, hitting him on the head with a folding chair.

Lester crumpled to the ground.

Beau hadn't left her after all. Lou dropped the knife onto the counter. Her fingers shook so much, she was glad she hadn't tried to use it. They both spun toward the windows as three Button Police Department cruisers came screeching to a stop next to Lester's car. Officers spilled out. Lou knocked on the glass to get their attention.

"We're in here," she called to them, motioning for them to come around back.

They burst into the kitchen, weapons drawn. She and Beau put up their hands, and an officer knelt to examine Lester.

"He's the one who killed Nina Upton. And I'm pretty sure he shot Judge Potts too," Lou blurted. "The weapons are both in a bag in his trunk. His car is parked right out there." She pointed behind her.

To Lou's horror, one officer grabbed Beau, bending his arms behind his back. He reached for the handcuffs on his belt.

"Stop," she cried out. "He had nothing to do with this. He saved me." Her tone had a pleading quality to it. "Let him go," Lou said more sternly this time, stepping toward the officer.

The officer frowned, but Easton stepped into the kitchen at that very moment and lifted his chin. "Jones, it's okay. You can trust her."

Officer Jones unlocked the handcuffs, and Lou reached forward much like Beau had earlier when she'd been hiding in the bush. After a moment of hesitation, Beau took her hand. They checked with Easton before Lou led Beau out of the house, over to an area of the curb where they were out of the way of the police.

"Thank you for your help, Beau," Lou said once they were sitting. She hadn't heard him speak yet, so it surprised her when he answered.

"You're welcome, Lou." His deep voice rumbled next to her.

He knew her name. She sucked in a quick breath as something clicked. The mystery texter had changed tone so drastically. What if it had been less about what she'd asked and more that it was a different person? There had been the stuff about not trusting his eyes or his brain. That hadn't been his uncle speaking.

"It was you. Wasn't it?" She gave him a sidelong glance.

"At first," he said. "Jonah talked about you and your book-shop all the time. I found your number in one of his phones once he went away. When I saw you get in trouble with the detective the day you found Nina's body, I thought I could help. But my uncle found the phone on Monday. He was the one who was trying to meet. I wanted to warn you, but I didn't know how."

Easton had been right. The killer had asked her to meet. It just wasn't who she'd been talking to that whole time.

"So you knew it was your uncle who killed Nina?" Lou asked.

He shook his head. "I had a feeling. Nina and Judge Potts. I saw someone jump Nina early in the morning, but I couldn't be sure."

"And you didn't feel you could go to the police yourself because of your history?" Lou guessed. Based on the cynicism and doubt she'd faced, she couldn't even imagine what they would've thought if someone who had been in trouble with the law before came in saying the same things. Feeling strongly that her last question was quite rhetorical, Lou added on something she felt needed saying. "I know they might not have believed you, but you should trust in yourself, Beau. You did a good thing today."

He studied his hands and lowered his chin. "My past isn't great. I know I messed up. I used to have anger issues, but I'm not dangerous like they say."

"Why did you say you couldn't trust your eyes or brain?" she asked.

"I take anxiety medication." He swallowed. "I changed to a new medicine last week, and sometimes the change is rough.

New meds sometimes mess with my concept of reality, especially when we're trying to get my dosage correct."

Lou smiled. "Well, I'm glad you reached out to me. You know, not everyone thinks that you're dangerous. Peggy Lee Milton said Benji really enjoyed having you around on the farm before he died."

Beau's gray eyes locked on to Lou's, and it looked like that meant a lot to him.

Footsteps clomped behind them, and Lou glanced behind her to find Noah racing over. "I saw your car parked at my house, and then I saw the police. Are you okay?" Noah pulled Lou into a tight hug when she stood.

"I'm fine," she said into his jacket. His surgery must've finished, and she hadn't been in any state to give him an update. Lou winced, thinking of the list of phone alerts she must have. "Beau saved me." She furrowed her eyebrows. "How did you have the keys to Nina's house?" she asked.

Beau tipped his head toward the small house. "I let Mr. Muffins out during the day for Nina while she was at work. I was going to stay over here and watch him when she was on her cruise last month, but then she ended up eating some bad casserole from someone at her work and got food poisoning, so she didn't go."

Lou pressed her lips together. So it had never been Devon's food truck that had gotten Nina sick in the first place. Lou was glad to hear it. Even though she didn't condone his idea to leave a threatening message, she knew the feeling of helplessness when up against someone as litigious as Nina was.

"And how was she connected to your brother's trial? What was your uncle getting back at her for?" Lou asked.

"I didn't know she was involved at all," Beau said.

"She wasn't," Easton said as he walked over to the group.

200

"Your uncle just confessed that he was returning from shooting Judge Potts, and Nina caught him stashing the murder weapon in the storm drain. He killed her merely because she was in the wrong place at the wrong time."

"And Uncle Lester would've known someone like Nina would never keep her mouth shut," Beau said, filling in the final reasoning.

"He took the leaves from in front of Chase's house and dumped them over her body to cover it up." Easton sighed. Already, Lou could tell a difference in his posture. His big case was solved. Actually, both local cases were solved.

She saw Detective Anderson standing off to the side, glaring over at her. Lou waved and smiled. He turned his back on her.

"I want to say we would've caught him anyway, since I just came from talking to Jonah at the prison upstate." Easton's gaze flicked up to meet Beau's. "Your cousin's really sorry about the theft he played a part in and wanted to change his ways. I asked him about the gun your uncle said was stolen. He said it never was. He reported it because Jonah tried to steal it for you. He said it was your father's before he passed away, and Jonah thought you deserved to have it, but your uncle found it before Jonah could give it to you. Lester conveniently never reported that it had been found."

Beau nodded. "That sounds like Jonah. He was always thinking of me. And it was a nice gesture, but I want nothing to do with guns, or my dad."

Sadness expanded inside Lou as she realized a lot of his trauma must've come at the hands of his deceased father. And then he went to live with yet another abusive male figure.

"Anyway," Easton continued, "I'm sorry I didn't take your call, Lou. I was driving here as quickly as I could."

Another officer called Easton over. He held up his index

finger and then turned back toward Lou and Beau. "If you two don't mind sticking around, I'd like to get your statements about what happened."

Lou told Easton to take his time, they would be there.

As they stood there waiting, Noah inhaled deeply and looked at Beau. "So, since you're so familiar with Mr. Muffins' needs, any chance you'd like to adopt him now that Nina's gone?"

Beau's gray eyes widened. They lit up with true happiness. "I'd love to."

CHAPTER 24

Lou grinned as Marigold situated Lou's pumpkin, the one she'd carved to look like a sleeping Sapphire, next to the white cat on the table in the bookshop. Marigold, dressed as none other than a cat dragon, giggled and then tugged on Noah's sweater, asking him to take a picture of the two Sapphires.

In addition to the pumpkin Sapphire and the real Sapphire, there was a large bowl of Halloween candy sitting on the book-shop table. The sun was just setting, and Lou knew the streets would be flooded with costumed locals wanting sweets within the hour.

Lou had quickly abandoned her idea of handing out books instead of candy, realizing how expensive that would be, and receiving a scolding from Willow about childhood expectations.

"You don't want to be one of those people who hand out toothpaste," Willow had argued.

Lou found it greatly offensive that anyone should compare

books to something as boring as toothpaste, but she let the comment go. It was no use. So, Lou had purchased candy and had it ready and waiting for the trick-or-treaters. She was rather proud of her cat costume … until Willow and Easton entered the bookshop. They'd dressed as Mother Earth and Father Time, and they looked fantastic. Their costumes were handmade, Willow having worked on them for months.

"You're cute as a button," Willow said, booping Lou on the black triangle nose she'd drawn on with makeup.

"And you're gorgeous." Lou pulled her friend into a hug, then she turned her attention to the front door as two more people entered.

Willow and Lou broke out into laughter.

"What?" Peggy Lee asked, placing her hands on her hips as she lifted her wart-covered prosthetic nose. "I'm a garden troll."

"You certainly are," Willow said through a chuckle, then she pulled Peggy Lee in for a hug.

Over the past week, the two of them had grown much closer. Even though it hadn't been the plan to involve Peggy Lee in the nursery, Willow was learning that Peggy Lee knew more about the running of a business than she did. After seeing how well they worked together, they'd started talking about a partnership rather than just a rental agreement.

Speaking of perfect partnerships, another one entered the bookshop behind Peggy Lee. Beau Frazier walked inside, cradling Mr. Muffins in his arm.

"And what are you two supposed to be?" Willow asked, eyeing the small slingshot connected to the Pomeranian's collar.

"David and Goliath," Beau said in his deep voice. His mouth curved into a smile.

He was smiling a lot more lately, especially once Peggy Lee

and Willow had offered him a job helping with work on the farm, and he had moved into Peggy Lee's spare bedroom. He and Mr. Muffins were getting along great with Peggy Lee and Holden Clawfield, especially since it looked as if Holden would surpass Mr. Muffins in height and weight sooner rather than later.

"Everyone ready?" Easton called as he noticed a group of local children walking up to the bookstore, their parents following behind.

The next hour was a blur, and Lou was happy she put her friends on candy duty because she wanted to keep the book-shop open. She'd put together a spooky selection of books, including Stephen King's *It*, in honor of Devon Goddard. And she'd sold more books in a few hours than she had previously that week.

She was just handing a woman her receipt when something startlingly familiar caught her attention. It was a purse, and sewn onto the exterior of the bag was the face of a creepy doll with legs hanging down and arms jutting out from the sides.

Lou glanced up at the woman who had the purse proudly displayed on her shoulder and the man holding her free hand. They slid a book each toward Lou for purchase. She cleared her throat and pretended to have just noticed the woman's purse.

"Oh, what an interesting piece. Where did you get it?" Lou asked as calmly as she could.

The man rolled his eyes, but the woman looked up at him in a universal *I told you so* expression. She beamed.

"I make them. Aren't they cool?" The woman held it forward so Lou could see the details.

"Creepy," the man said through a cough.

Ignoring him, Lou dug further, needing answers. "I thought I saw something like it last week in the corn maze off Linen

Drive. Is this a one-of-a-kind piece or..." Lou left the sentence hanging so this woman might fill in the ending.

She slapped her hand on her knee. "Oh my goodness. Yes, Hank and I were there last week. It was the scariest thing."

Lou leaned forward.

"I got to the end of that maze before I realized that I'd dropped her. I went back through, tracing my steps, and I found her. Thank goodness." The woman leaned into Hank and patted his chest. "My hero broke the rules and went right through those stalks to grab her for me. Though, I think he scared the daylights out of some poor woman. He didn't realize she was there until he saw her running away."

"That was me!" Lou almost felt like laughing, but here was just one more thing bugging her. "Do you name the purses? Because I swear I heard someone calling out a name. Something like Nina?"

The woman placed a hand on her chest and said, "Oh, my name is Tina. Maybe that's what you heard. I lost the purse, and then Henry lost me. He was calling my name for a while before he found me."

Lou placed Tina and Henry's books in a bag, and they handed over the payment. "Well, I hope you have a wonderful Halloween," Lou said with a wave.

"We will. Do you want me to leave my card in case you ever want a purse for yourself?" Tina asked.

Lou nodded, not sure how to say no.

Willow came over and hooked an arm around Lou's shoulders as they left. "Going to buy yourself a doll-head purse?" she teased, having obviously eavesdropped on the conversation.

"Not anytime soon. But at least the mystery of the corn maze is solved." She sighed. "In fact, every mystery that's been plaguing my thoughts over the past couple of weeks is officially now solved."

Willow rubbed at her stomach. "I've got one more mystery for you to figure out."

"What's that?" Lou asked with a smirk.

"What piece of candy should I eat next?" She wiggled her fingers over the bowl.

Lou picked out a chocolate for herself while Willow unwrapped something gummy-looking. Then she picked up the bowl as another round of trick-or-treaters entered the bookshop.

WHISKERS AND WORDS WILL RETURN ...

Pick up the fifth book in the series.

In this Christmas story, there is no happy ending for Scrooge.

Louisa Henry has read the Dickens classic enough times to spot a Scrooge when she sees one. Arthur Crawford is as sour as they come. Even worse? There's no chance for his redemption because during the town's Christmas tree lighting, his body is found suspended in the lights of the largest pine.

No one is surprised that Arthur's selfish ways finally caught up to him. But when it becomes apparent that the killer won't stop, Lou must delve deep into Arthur's Christmases past to find out who took away his Christmas future.

Buy it now!

Join Eryn Scott's mailing list to learn about new releases and sales!

STONEYBROOK MYSTERIES

Ongoing series * Farmers market * Recipes * Crime solving twins * Cats!

Whiskers and Words Mysteries

Ongoing series * Best friends *
Bookshop full of cats

About the Author

Eryn Scott lives in the Pacific Northwest with her husband and their quirky animals. She loves classic literature, musicals, knitting, and hiking. She writes cozy mysteries and women's fiction. Join her mailing list to learn about new releases and sales!

www.erynscott.com